STAR OF THE SHOW

The club president looked around the bleachers and smiled. "I won't keep you in suspense any longer," she said. "The theme of this year's fall show is—'Under the Sea.'"

Some of the skaters clapped, and a few of the boys groaned.

"Now, let me run down some of the numbers the show committee has come up with," Mrs. Bowen said.

Tori threw up her hands. "This is killing me," she whispered to Danielle. "When is she going to announce the solo?"

Finally, after Mrs. Bowen had described every single number, she said, "And now for our featured solo skater. The role of the Sea Queen will be skated by—"

Danielle heard Tori draw in her breath in anticipation of the next two words.

"Danielle Panati!"

Silver Blades

titles in Large-Print Editions:

IN THE
SPOTLIGHT

Melissa Lowell

Created by Parachute Press

Gareth Stevens Publishing
MILWAUKEE

For a free color catalog describing Gareth Stevens' list of high-quality books and multimedia programs, call 1-800-542-2595 (USA) or 1-800-461-9120 (Canada). Gareth Stevens Publishing's Fax: (414) 225-0377. See our catalog, too, on the World Wide Web: http://gsinc.com

Library of Congress Cataloging-in-Publication Data

Lowell, Melissa.
   In the spotlight / Melissa Lowell.
     p. cm. — (Silver blades; #2)
   Summary: When Danielle lands the lead role in the ice show and she begins to act strangely, her friends suspect that she may be afraid of being in the spotlight.
   ISBN 0-8368-2064-9 (lib. bdg.)
   [1. Ice skating—Fiction. 2. Self-confidence—Fiction.]
   I. Title. II. Series: Lowell, Melissa. Silver blades; #2.
PZ7.L96456In 1998
[Fic]—dc21   97-39609

First published in this edition in 1998 by
Gareth Stevens Publishing
1555 North RiverCenter Drive, Suite 201
Milwaukee, WI 53212 USA

Printed in the United States of America

1 2 3 4 5 6 7 8 9 02 01 00 99 98

IN THE SPOTLIGHT

"**D**anielle!" someone called as Danielle Panati entered the locker room of the Seneca Valley Ice Arena. "Over here!"

Danielle smiled when she spotted her friend Jill Wong. She and Jill had been close friends for the past two years, ever since Danielle had joined Silver Blades, one of the best skating clubs in the entire country. Jill had been a member for three years, and now she was one of the most advanced skaters in the club.

Danielle had worked very hard to make it into Silver Blades—it had taken her almost two years of constant practicing. Then she'd had to go through a grueling audition in front of the two Silver Blades coaches, Franz Weiler and Kathy Bart, both former championship skaters themselves. The whole ordeal had been worth it, because now Danielle was actually on her way to becoming a top class skater. Six days a week, with the other members of Silver Blades, Danielle practiced for long hours on the ice, took special dance lessons and weight training, and participated in competitions.

Jill was sitting on a bench in the corner, lacing her skates. She wore bright red leg warmers over her flesh-colored tights, and a cherry-red sweater and skirt. Her long black braid was held back with red barrettes and bright red ribbon.

Beside Jill was Nikki Simon, one of the newest members of Silver Blades. Nikki looked up and grinned as Danielle approached, revealing a set of braces. Nikki had a dark green headband over her dark brown hair, and she was wearing her light blue Silver Blades warm-up jacket. It was five forty-five on a cold October morning.

"Hi, Dani," Nikki said. "You're kind of late this morning."

Danielle put down her skate bag and fished out a polka-dot ponytail holder for her long honey-brown hair. "I know—I was up late studying and I slept through my alarm," she said with a sigh.

"Well, you're not the only one who's late," said Jill cheerfully. "Tori just walked in."

A short, pretty girl with curly blond hair and pale blue eyes was headed toward the nearest empty bench by the door. Behind her was her mother, a tall, attractive blond woman in a long cashmere coat. Mrs. Carsen came to almost every skating practice Tori had—Danielle couldn't ever remember *not* seeing her at the rink. Tori had been skating competitively since she was eight, and her mother obviously had big plans for her.

"And I don't want to see you dawdling with your friends today," Mrs. Carsen said in a loud, raspy voice. Danielle had never met anyone as obnoxious as Mrs. Carsen—she was always yelling at Tori in front of other people, and today was no exception. All the skaters in the dressing room turned to look at her. "It's bad enough that you forgot your skating bag and we had to go back home and get it."

"Poor Tori," Nikki whispered. "I'd hate it if my mother nagged me so much."

"Me too," Danielle whispered back. "Do you think we should go over and say hi?"

"No," said Jill. "It would just make things worse."

Danielle felt terrible for their friend as Mrs. Carsen continued to scold. "The fall ice show is coming up in less than a month," she went on, pulling the rubber guards from her daughter's skates. "How are you ever going to get chosen for the big solo spot at this rate? Just think of all that time and money we've been spending. From now on, you can't afford to be even one minute late." With that, Mrs. Carsen swept dramatically out of the locker room, leaving everyone staring after her.

"She should have been an actress, not a skater,"

Jill whispered to Danielle. Mrs. Carsen had been a competitive figure skater before Tori was born.

Tori quickly turned to face the wall and furiously began to lace her skates. In less than two minutes she was headed toward the ice, without saying anything to anyone else in the room.

"Phew!" Jill said as she, Danielle, and Nikki filed out of the dressing room with the other skaters. "I've never heard Mrs. Carsen so upset."

"It must be the show," Danielle said. "Tori's mom is putting a lot of pressure on her to get picked for the solo this year."

Every year Silver Blades put on two big ice shows, one in the fall and one in the spring. For each show, one member was selected to perform a special number for the show's finale. Diana Mitchell, the best skater in Silver Blades, had skated the solo last spring. Lately everyone had been speculating about who would be chosen for the solo this time. A lot of skaters wanted the part—especially Tori.

Danielle followed her friends out to the rink, feeling the familiar blast of cold air as she stepped through the glass doors that led to the ice surface. The Seneca Hills Ice Arena was practically Danielle's second home. It contained two Olympic-sized rinks under the same roof, one for figure skating, and the other for hockey. The arena also had a snack bar, a small pro shop, a weight room, and several small offices.

As Danielle skated out onto the ice, she considered her own chances of being chosen for the solo by the club board. Even though Danielle wanted to be selected as much as anyone else, she didn't think it would happen—at least not for this show. She knew she was a good skater but not a great one. Mr. Weiler was always telling her that she had lots of potential, if only she would start developing her own special style—and maybe lose a few pounds. Danielle had heard so much about potential that sometimes she wondered if she could ever live up to it. What good was potential if she couldn't do anything with it? For now, she'd just have to root for one of her best friends to get the solo.

"No, no, no!" Mr. Weiler called across the rink, accentuating each "no" with a clap of his thick brown leather gloves. "You're not concentrating, Danielle. Take it again!"

Danielle frowned as she picked herself up from the ice. Somehow she'd managed to fall over her own feet on a tricky footwork sequence of steps and turns across the rink. Now the back of her black skating skirt was completely wet, and she could feel a run starting down her tights. The morning practice was not going well.

"Focus this time!" Mr. Weiler instructed.

Danielle glanced around at the other skaters whizzing past her as she took her place at the far corner of the rink. She wanted to make sure she had enough room before she started. She launched into the footwork sequence for what felt like the fifteenth time, biting her lip in concentration. Three-turn, back three, step, mohawk. Turn, step—THUD!

Danielle collided with another skater and fell onto the ice.

"Hey, watch where you're going!" Bobby Rodgers said, rubbing his shoulder as he stood up. "You could have killed me." Bobby was a thin, blond ninth-grader.

"Sorry," Danielle said. "But I'm on lesson." Everyone knew that a skater working with his or her coach had the right-of-way.

"Well, you should still look out," Bobby grumbled, skating away.

Danielle glanced back over her shoulder. Mr. Weiler didn't look very happy as he rocked back and forth on the blades of his black leather skates. She'd have to try the sequence again.

She sighed and took her place back in the corner. This time she got through the footwork without bumping into anyone, even though she had to maneuver around Diana Mitchell, who was spinning at center ice. Most of the skaters automatically got out of Diana's way, even when they were on lesson, because she never looked out for anyone else. As the best skater in the club, she seemed to think it was her privilege.

Mr.Weiler gave Danielle a big smile as she skated up. He even lifted his fur cap in a salute, revealing his shiny bald head. "That was much better," he said.

"I think you are ready to try your whole program now, with the music."

Danielle bit her lip. She'd been having a lot of problems with her routine lately, and she wasn't at all sure it was good enough to show Mr. Weiler yet. She hated it when anyone, especially her coach, saw anything she did before it was absolutely perfect. But at Silver Blades, perfection was rare—Danielle had a much better chance of getting a 100 on a vocabulary test in school.

Mr. Weiler looked up at the big clock on the hockey scoreboard at the other end of the arena. "Let's go, Danielle, or we'll be cutting into Tori's lesson time."

Danielle skated across the ice to the Plexiglas-enclosed booth where the tape player was located. Several skaters were already in line with their cassettes.

"You go ahead, Danielle," Jill said. "You're still on lesson, right?"

"Yeah," Danielle said, popping her tape into the player. "Mr. Weiler wants to see my whole program. I wish it were better."

"You'll do fine," Jill said. "I saw your program last weekend—it looked great. Knock him dead!" she called as Danielle left the booth.

"Thanks!" Danielle said over her shoulder as she skated toward center ice. She wished she felt as good about her routine as Jill did. Sometimes she couldn't believe she and Jill were such good friends—they were so different. Jill was so confident; she never let anything stand in her way or get her down. Danielle really admired that about her friend.

Remember what Jill said, Danielle told herself, glancing at Mr. Weiler to see if he was ready. Knock him dead. She struck her opening pose and waited for her music to begin, trying to forget that anyone was watching her. She skated better when she was alone or only with friends.

After a sudden burst of static from the tape, Danielle heard the beep that signaled the start of her program. She had picked the music, several short sections from *The Nutcracker*, with Mr. Weiler's help. Just hearing her favorite classical pieces, especially "The Waltz of the Flowers," always made her feel better.

She pushed off and began to lose herself in her routine. She circled the rink to the music, carefully covering the entire ice surface. Like all figure skaters' programs, Danielle's had been carefully designed to balance an equal number of jumps and spins with footwork and slower sections that allowed her to catch her breath.

This time she landed jump after jump and centered all of her spins. The other skaters, even Diana, scrambled to get out of her way, and the troublesome footwork sequence went unusually well. Danielle did falter a bit on one of her double jump combinations, two-footing the double toe loop, but she quickly recovered and went on. She sensed everyone watching her as she finished her program with a blinding scratch spin, and struck her final pose as the last cymbal clashed.

Someone clapped, and she heard Nikki call, "Nice going, Danielle!"

She skated back to Mr. Weiler, feeling very hopeful, but her coach's face held no expression. "So, uh, what did you think?" Danielle asked nervously.

Mr. Weiler smiled. "I think your routine is coming together very nicely. As a matter of fact, it's some of the best skating I've ever seen you do." He nodded. "Nice job, Danielle."

Danielle had to hold on to the barrier to keep from falling over. Mr. Weiler had never said anything so complimentary to her before. "Thanks," she said.

"Keep practicing, and I'll see you this afternoon." Mr. Weiler skated off to begin his next private lesson, with Tori, and Danielle stood on the ice for a moment, still in a state of shock.

Had her routine really been that good? She still wasn't sure how she had done it, but she wanted to remember—so she could do the same thing the next time!

"**Y**our program looked really good today," Nikki told Danielle as they took off their skates in the locker room after practice later that morning before school.

"Thanks," Danielle said. "I think I was lucky—Mr. Weiler was in a great mood."

Jill shook her head. "His mood has nothing to do with it," she said firmly. "You skated a great routine. You just need a little more confidence, Danielle."

"That's easy for you to say," Danielle told her. "You were *born* confident. You love it when people watch you skate, and you're never shy with anyone."

"That's because I'm used to having so many people around me," Jill said. "How would you like to have six younger brothers and sisters?"

"No, thanks," Danielle said. "One older brother is

enough." She considered her brother, Nicholas, to be one of the most obnoxious people on the entire planet.

Nikki laughed. "Oh, come on, Jill. Your family is the greatest. Everyone's always talking and laughing and running around at your house." Nikki was an only child, and she often said she was envious of all the activity at the Wongs'.

"What are you guys talking about?" Tori asked, walking over with her skating bag. She was already dressed for school.

"Cool outfit, Tori," Nikki said.

Tori glanced down at her black-and-purple over-sized sweater and matching purple short skirt. "Oh, this is nothing," she said. "My mom got it for me on sale."

Danielle and Jill exchanged glances. Tori always had the nicest outfits, but she acted as though they were rags. She claimed that everyone at Kent Academy, the private school she attended, wore much better clothes. Sometimes Danielle had a feeling that Tori would rather be going to Grandview Middle School, with her and Nikki and Jill, but Mrs. Carsen wouldn't hear of it. Her daughter had to have the "best" of everything.

Danielle knew that Nikki was making a real effort to be nice to Tori—they'd had some problems getting along when Nikki first moved to town two months ago. Fortunately they'd worked things out between them, and they were becoming friends.

Tori dropped down onto the bench as the other

girls finished dressing and doing their hair. "I'm sorry I couldn't really talk to you guys earlier this morning," she said. "My mom was kind of crazy about me being late and all. She's getting all worked up over this dumb show and—"

"That's okay," Danielle interrupted her. She hated to see Tori so upset and apologetic when it wasn't her fault. "We understand."

"So when do you think they'll finally announce the theme of this show?" Nikki asked, running a brush through her hair. "It's getting kind of late, isn't it? Isn't the show in five weeks?"

"The club board members always keep the theme a secret until practically the last minute," Jill explained. "Then they make a big announcement about the numbers everyone will be in and who'll be skating the final solo."

By now the dressing room was practically empty. Most of the other Silver Blades members had already left for school.

"Hurry up, Danielle," Jill scolded as Danielle lingered at one of the small mirrors, trying to work her ponytail holder back into her hair. "The rest of us are ready to go."

"She has to get her hair just right," Nikki teased her. "In case she sees *Jordan* later."

Danielle blushed. She thought Jordan McShane was the cutest boy at Grandview Middle School, and she'd had a crush on him for ages. Her friends loved to tease her about him, even though Jordan, an eighth-grader, probably didn't even know she existed.

"I know how you can meet Jordan," Jill said. "Dani, have you ever thought about switching from figure skating to ice hockey?"

Then she, Nikki, and Tori burst out laughing.

"Cut it out, you guys!" Danielle said, hiding a smile as she quickly stuffed the ponytail holder back into her jacket pocket.

"Maybe you guys can learn to skate pairs together," Tori teased. "Or better yet, how about ice dancing? Imagine how romantic it would be . . . ." She took Danielle's arms and started waltzing around the locker room with her.

Danielle laughed as Tori tried to lower her into a dip, and nearly dropped her. "A lot more romantic than this!" Danielle cried.

"Is that what you're having for breakfast?"

Danielle looked up from her science textbook. "Oh, hi, Mom," she said. It was Tuesday, and Danielle was trying to finish her reading assignment before morning practice.

Mrs. Panati, a small woman with dark brown hair, frowned at the chocolate-frosted doughnut on Danielle's plate. "You need to go skate for two hours," she reminded her. "You should be having a more nutritious breakfast."

"I'm not that hungry, Mom," Danielle protested. "This is fine."

Mrs. Panati sighed and looked up at the kitchen clock. "Honey, it's five-twenty already. We're going to have to leave for the rink now if you want to make your early-morning practice."

"Five-twenty already?" Danielle slammed her book shut and jumped up from her chair. "Let's go."

Danielle's grandmother emerged from her bedroom off the kitchen, tightening the belt of her flowered bathrobe. "Two hours of skating, a full day of school, and then more skating. Sometimes I think you're crazy, Danielle." She smiled and rubbed her eyes.

Danielle gave her a quick hug. "Maybe I am, Grandma, but if I can keep it up, you might see me in the Olympics someday." She was feeling very positive about her skating, after what Mr. Weiler had said the day before.

"I'd better," Grandma Panati said. "I don't get up at five in the morning for just anybody, you know." She smiled at Danielle.

"Time to go, Danielle," Mrs. Panati said. "Why don't you go back to sleep, Mother. I'll see you later."

Danielle quickly gathered her jacket, knapsack, and skating bag and headed toward the door, almost knocking over a chair in her haste.

"Hold it right there, Danielle Marie!" Grandma Panati called. "You're not going without this." She grabbed a banana from the fruit bowl on the kitchen table and handed it to Danielle. "You can eat this on the way."

"Okay, okay," Danielle mumbled. She tucked the

banana into her jacket pocket and gave her grandmother a peck on the cheek. " 'Bye, Grandma."

As soon as Danielle got into the car, she took out
her book again.

"Do you have a test today?" Mrs. Panati asked.

Danielle nodded. "I was trying to get in some last-
minute cramming for a quiz this afternoon," she said.

Danielle's mother pulled out of the driveway. "You
know, honey, I wish you'd pay more attention to what
you're eating. You shouldn't eat a chocolate doughnut
for breakfast."

"Nicholas eats chocolate doughnuts all the time,"
Danielle said.

"Your brother eats plenty of everything, not just
junk food," Mrs. Panati pointed out.

"He's a bottomless pit," Danielle grumbled. "He eats
everything in sight and doesn't gain an ounce. It isn't
fair."

"Well," Mrs. Panati said, "it's different for Nicholas.
He doesn't have to watch his weight the way you do."

"What's that supposed to mean?" Danielle asked,
an edge creeping into her voice "Am I too fat or
something? Don't I get enough exercise, skating five
hours a day?"

"Of course you're not fat," Mrs. Panati said, turn-
ing onto Grandview Avenue. The Seneca Valley Ice
Arena was only a few miles away, toward downtown.
"I worry about *what* you eat, not how much."

"I eat just fine," Danielle muttered. Deep down she
knew her mother was right. She did eat too much

junk food and she was a little self-conscious about her weight. Mr. Weiler's warning that a few extra pounds could spoil a skater's graceful line on the ice and make it harder to get enough height on jumps rang in her ears. All the skaters in Silver Blades had to be conscious about not getting too heavy.

"Let's talk about this later," Mrs. Panati said as she turned the car into the parking lot of the office complex where the arena was located. "I've got to get back home so I can get to work early today. I'm making a big presentation to a client this morning."

Danielle breathed a sigh of relief. Since her mom worked full-time at a small advertising agency, she didn't have a lot of extra time to lecture her children, the way Tori's mother did.

On her way into the rink Danielle took the banana her grandmother had given her and tossed it into a trash can outside the door. She didn't like eating fruit. What was so bad about one little doughnut, anyway?

"Danielle, guess what?" Tori said when Danielle walked over to the rink's edge a few minutes later. "Mrs. Bowen's called a meeting for all club members right after practice this afternoon!"

Danielle sat down on a bench and quickly laced her skates. Mrs. Bowen was the club president. Her son, Mitchell, was also a member of Silver Blades.

"You know what that means," Jill added. "She's going to announce the theme of the fall show!"

"And the name of the soloist," Tori put in.

"What do you guys think the theme of the show will be?" asked Nikki.

"I have no idea," said Danielle, stepping onto the ice. "But a carnival theme might be fun."

"We did the circus last year," Tori reminded her as the group started circling the rink together.

"Maybe it'll be something like 'Winter Wonderland,'" Nikki suggested.

Jill groaned. "How corny! That sounds like a theme the club board members would come up with, all right."

"How about 'Salute to the Olympics'?" Danielle put in.

"Not bad," Tori said, nodding. "Too bad they don't ask us what *we* want to do for the show." Then she glanced up into the stands. Danielle saw Mrs. Carsen already settled with a woolen blanket over her knees and a steaming thermos of coffee. "I'd better go," Tori told them. "I have to run through my program before my lesson with Mr. Weiler."

Danielle watched her friend skate over to the sound booth. She couldn't imagine having to perform under so much pressure all the time. If Tori didn't get the solo, her mother would probably be furious with her.

I may not be the best skater, but at least I don't have all that pressure to deal with, Danielle thought. She knew she couldn't handle it even half as well as Tori did.

That afternoon Danielle was thinking about the ice show again as she walked to her locker after school. She kept trying to guess what the theme of this show would be and what role she would have. She had heard a rumor about some pairs skating this year—what if she was picked to skate with somebody she didn't like? Out of the twenty-six Silver Blades members only ten were boys—not great odds of being paired up with someone good.

Danielle turned down the hall to her locker. She had to get all the books she needed for homework that night before she went to the rink. Trying to memorize the twenty vocabulary words for her English quiz tomorrow as she walked, Danielle stared at the floor and repeated each word to herself. When she finally looked up, there was Jordan McShane—standing in front of her locker!

3

Danielle stood frozen to the spot, not knowing what to do. Why was Jordan waiting at her locker?

Suddenly he glanced up and flashed her an apologetic grin. "Sorry," he said. "Is this your locker? I was looking at the math test I just got back, and I wasn't paying attention." He held out the test to Danielle. "Ninety-two, can you believe it?"

Danielle smiled. "Congratulations," she said. "That's great."

Jordan moved aside, and Danielle began to dial her combination, trying to hide her embarrassment. For a minute she'd actually believed that Jordan was waiting for her.

Jordan ran a hand through his dark brown hair. "You're Nicholas Panati's sister, aren't you? I'm friends with Nicholas. We're on the hockey team—the Seneca Hills Hawks—together."

"Yeah, I'm his sister," Danielle said. "Actually everyone always thinks we look like twins." Inwardly she cringed. What was she talking about? She sounded like an idiot.

Jordan nodded. "You guys do look a lot alike. I've seen you around at the rink. You're a pretty good skater."

"Thanks," Danielle said, relaxing a bit.

"Hey, are you heading over to the arena now? I usually take the bus, but today my brother's driving me over. Do you want a ride?"

"Uh . . . that would be great," Danielle said. Incredibly great, she thought. "But my grandmother's driving Nicholas and me today."

Jordan shrugged. "Okay," he said. He started walking away down the hall. "See you around."

"See you at the rink!" Danielle called after him, but she wasn't sure he heard her. With a sigh she pulled open her locker. The picture of Olympic skating medalist Nancy Kerrigan that she'd clipped from *Skating* magazine and taped to the inside of the door caught her eye.

Danielle gazed at the photo. Nancy looked so graceful and confident, just the way she herself had always wanted to be. The famous skater had her leg extended behind her in a classic arabesque—or spiral, as it was called in skating—and she was smiling out at her audience.

The ice show! Danielle had been in such a daze since her run-in with Jordan that she'd forgotten all about the club meeting at the rink.

Nicholas was already in the passenger seat of Grandma Panati's rattly old red Volvo station wagon when Danielle ran down the school's side steps to the parking lot. "Move it, Tubs!" he yelled, sticking his head out the window. Danielle stopped dead in her tracks, wanting to sink straight through the pavement. Nervously she glanced around the parking lot. Had anyone heard her brother call her "Tubs," her childhood nickname?

Luckily the parking lot was nearly empty, and Jordan was nowhere in sight.

Breathing a sigh of relief, Danielle yanked open the car door and slid into the backseat. "Hi, Grandma," she said.

"What's up, Tubs?" Nicholas said cheerfully.

"Don't call me that," Danielle growled, clobbering her brother over the back of his head with her knapsack full of books.

"Ow!" Nicholas cried, clutching his neck. "That hurt."

"Good," Danielle said. She slumped back in the seat and crossed her arms as the Volvo pulled out of the parking lot.

"I don't see what the big deal is," Nicholas complained, twisting around in the front seat. "You're not as fat as you were a few years ago, so why should you care?"

Danielle glared at him, not bothering to talk again until they'd reached the rink. Nicholas could be such a jerk sometimes.

"Have fun, you two," Grandma Panati said when Danielle and Nicholas got out of the car a few minutes later. "See you tonight!" She waved at them, and the Volvo rattled off, out of the parking lot.

Inside the arena Nicholas turned toward the boys' locker room, and Danielle headed into the girls' locker room. It was practically empty. Everyone must already be on the ice, Danielle thought.

After changing into her practice clothes Danielle headed to the ballet barre that was installed near the entrance to the ice. Mr. Weiler was always complaining that his skaters didn't do enough stretching exercises. She saw him speaking with Tori on the other side of the rink. Nikki and Jill were on the ice practicing jumps. Danielle couldn't wait to tell her friends she'd talked to Jordan, but this wasn't exactly the best time. She could just imagine Mr. Weiler saying in his German accent, "Danielle, what is so important that you need to interrupt our practice here? Skating comes before boys, you know."

Danielle did a few light kneebends, then brought her right leg up onto the barre and reached out over it with a graceful sweep of her arm. Feeling the pull on the back of her leg muscles, she switched arms and began to reach back in the opposite direction, being careful not to lock her knees. She continued to do the warm-up exercises she had learned during her three years of ballet lessons.

"What are you, a flamingo?" a familiar voice called.

Danielle snapped back up so quickly that she almost gave herself a whiplash. Sure enough, there was her stupid brother, standing by the soft-drink machine, laughing. And right beside him was Jordan. The two boys were suited up for practice, carrying helmets, huge gloves, and hockey sticks covered in black tape.

Gathering every possible ounce of dignity, Danielle took her leg off the barre and headed straight for the ice. Without a backward glance she pushed off onto the wet, newly resurfaced ice.

But before she could catch herself, Danielle's skates slipped out from underneath her, and she fell, her rear end crashing onto the ice. Danielle slid halfway to center ice before she finally came to a stop right in front of Mr. Weiler's black skates.

4

"**M**s. Panati, are you all right?" Danielle's coach said, looking down at her with great concern. "That was quite a show." He extended a hand to help her up as several other skaters came over to see what had happened. It wasn't unusual for anyone to fall, of course, but Danielle hadn't had time to fall correctly. You were supposed to tuck yourself into a ball to lessen the impact.

By now it seemed as if the entire club had gathered around Danielle. Jill's hand covered her mouth, and Danielle could see she was trying not to laugh. She supposed it would be kind of funny—if it had happened to someone else.

"Danielle, your guards!" Tori said, pointing.

Danielle looked down and groaned. In her haste to

get onto the ice, she had forgotten to remove the rubber guards from her blades. No wonder she'd wiped out like that!

Danielle ducked her head and quickly removed the skate guards. "I'm fine, really," she told everyone, blushing as she got to her feet and brushed the snowy ice from her tights. Actually she could feel a huge bruise starting on her hip, and her skating dress was soaking wet. She was going to kill Nicholas when she got home.

The crowd soon drifted away. Danielle, her cheeks still flaming, began to circle the ice faster and faster. She couldn't believe she'd fallen right in front of Jordan. He must think I'm a total klutz, Danielle thought.

Feeling the breeze against her face as she picked up more and more speed gradually made Danielle feel a little better. Soon she was landing some of her hardest jumps, even her double loop. For that jump she launched into the air from a backward position on the outside edge of her right skate blade. Then she had to snap her arms and legs into a tucked position and complete two full turns in the air.

After she was completely warmed up, Danielle went through her program without the music twice. Every now and then she felt Mr. Weiler watching her, but she pretended not to notice. She was sure he caught the nearly perfect double salchow jump she placed directly under his nose, though. The double salchow, for which she had to make a quick turn and take off backward from her right inside edge, was one of her best jumps.

Danielle knew she was showing off a bit, but Jill was right: She needed more confidence. Hard work and concentration were what had gotten her this far in her skating already. She might not have as much natural talent as some of the other members of Silver Blades, Danielle told herself, but she had plenty of determination.

"All right, people." Mrs. Bowen, the president of Silver Blades, clapped her hands for silence. "Let's begin our meeting now. We have some very important business to take care of in a very short time."

"That's for sure," Nikki said to Danielle. "Five weeks—to prepare for a huge show?"

Danielle shrugged. "I know. We're definitely cutting it close."

Mrs. Bowen smiled and waited for all of the skaters to quiet down as Kathy and Mr. Weiler took their seats in the front of the bleachers. Mrs. Graves, who was always in charge of costumes, was standing next to Mrs. Bowen, and on the other side of the Silver Blades president was Mr. Beekman, who had built the scenery for the show last spring.

"As you know," the club president began, "it is time for us to start preparing for our Silver Blades Fall Ice Spectacular."

The skaters began to clap, and Paul Delaney and Bobby Rodgers whistled loudly from the middle of the bleachers.

Mrs. Bowen held up one gloved hand. "Quiet, please," she said, frowning.

"Just get on with it," Tori muttered under her breath. She looks almost as nervous as her mom, Danielle thought. Danielle knew how much Tori wanted the solo, and for Tori's sake she hoped her friend would get it. Maybe then her mother would finally get off her back.

Mrs. Bowen gave a short speech, telling the seven new members of Silver Blades about the semiannual ice show. "The shows raise a good deal of money for the club," she said, "all of which goes to pay for your ice time, competition fees, travel, and coaching. This fall we're expecting everyone—skaters and parents—to become involved. We'll need people to sell tickets, make posters, sell advertising space in our show program, paint backdrops, help with costumes—and anything else you can do.

"As you may know," Mrs. Bowen continued, "we'll be running on a very short schedule this year. The Regional championships are being held in January, and the Silver Blades members who are attending this major competition will need to start training for it immediately after our show. That means, of course, that everyone will have to work even harder, but I'm sure that you will all have plenty of fun too."

By now Kelly O'Reilly and a few of the other younger skaters were becoming restless, shifting and turn-ing around in their seats. The club president looked around the bleachers and smiled. "I won't keep you in suspense any longer," she said. "The theme of this year's fall show is—'Under the Sea.'"

Some of the skaters clapped, and a few of the boys groaned.

"Let's do a rap show instead," Paul Delaney called out.

"An underwater ice show?" Nikki said, giggling. "We'll have to melt down the ice."

"Shhh!" Tori said, leaning forward in her seat.

"Now, let me run down some of the numbers the show committee has come up with," Mrs. Bowen said.

Tori threw up her hands. "This is killing me," she whispered to Danielle. "When is she going to announce the solo?"

"She's probably saving it for last," Danielle said.

Mrs. Bowen consulted her clipboard. "We'll begin with a grand parade of sea creatures," she said, adjusting her glasses slightly on her nose, "followed by a starfish number for some of our younger mem-bers, a mermaids' dance for the intermediate girls, a rock-lobster group number, and jumping fish for the boys. All of the older girls will be ocean waves in the traditional team precision number. And then, we'll have Jill Wong, Nikki Simon, Tori Carsen, and Danielle Panati skating with Steve Jenner, Alex Beekman, Josh Buskirk, and Mitchell Bowen in a special group pairs sailor number."

Danielle, Tori, and Nikki exchanged startled glances, and Jill, who was sitting a few rows below them, buried her face in her mittens. None of them had ever skated pairs, even for fun, because they were so busy with their own singles training. And the male members of Silver Blades were all at very different skating levels, since there were fewer of them.

"And now," Mrs. Bowen went on, turning to smile at the coaches behind her, "for our featured solo skater. The role of the Sea Queen will be skated by—"

Danielle heard Tori draw in her breath in anticipation of the next two words.

"Danielle Panati!"

5

Me? Danielle thought. They want me? She couldn't believe it. She felt as though she were in a fog, until Nikki leaned over and gave her a big hug.

"Congratulations!" Nikki said warmly.

"That's great, Danielle," Tori said. "I'm really happy for you." Danielle could tell that her friend was very disappointed, but Tori gave her a big smile.

Danielle saw Jill jumping up and down a few rows in front of them in the bleachers, waving her arms. "All right, Danielle!" she shouted. Other skaters called their congratulations to her.

Mrs. Bowen called for order, and the skaters settled down as she began to make more announcements about the show.

Danielle hardly heard one word that the club president was saying. Mrs. Bowen could have been on the moon, for all she knew.

She was lost in her own thoughts, picturing herself finishing her solo, throwing her arms up toward the bright overhead lights. The crowd would erupt into applause, and after she skated off the ice, she would accept a large bouquet of roses as flashbulbs went off all around her.

"Who *is* that skater?" people would ask, straining to get a closer look at Danielle. "She's going to be the next Olympic champion."

Suddenly everyone from Silver Blades started getting up from their seats, and Danielle realized with a start that the meeting was over.

"Better get a move on, Sea Queen," Nikki teased. "Mrs. Graves is going to start measuring us all for costumes in ten minutes."

"Oh, right," Danielle said, shaking herself out of her daze.

"Can you believe we're going to be skating a pairs number?" Nikki said as she, Danielle, and Tori walked down from the bleachers, stepping carefully in their skates. "How did they ever come up with such a crazy idea? We're singles skaters. We know nothing about skating pairs."

"Well, I think it's going to be awful," Tori said with a sigh. "Who wants to skate with the guys in Silver Blades?"

"They're not all bad, Tori," Nikki commented. "Besides, any kind of skating in front of a big audience will be good experience for all of us."

Jill caught up with them at the bottom of the bleachers. "I'm so glad they picked you," she said, throwing her arms around Danielle. "You're going to be so terrific! Aren't you excited?"

Danielle nodded. "Actually I'm more like stunned, shocked, surprised, stupefied—"

"Miss Vocabulary here," Nikki joked. "You can stop trying to impress us now." She squeezed Danielle's arm and smiled.

"Hey, let's get out of here," Jill said. "Maybe we can go grab a hot chocolate and celebrate before our rides show up."

"No, we can't," Tori said. "Don't you remember— we're supposed to get fitted for costumes with Mrs. Graves now. I wonder what we have to wear for the pairs number."

"Sailor outfits," Jill said, making a face.

"Please don't tell me we'll have to wear caps." Nikki groaned. "I look ridiculous in a cap."

"Not as ridiculous as I'm going to look in a bright red shell and claws for that rock-lobster number," Tori put in.

Danielle was barely paying attention to their conversation. She didn't care what she wore for the pairs number. What about her solo? Everyone in the entire rink was going to be watching *her*. What if I look stupid? she thought. What if I forget to take off my skate guards that night too?

All four girls headed for the locker room. Inside, Mrs. Graves had just finished taking down Diana's measurements. "Same as last year," the seamstress said. "Thank you."

"Dani, you go first," Jill said. "Maybe she'll tell you what your costume will be like."

Danielle walked up to Mrs. Graves, who was standing by the full-length mirror, tape measure in hand. "Hello there," the petite gray-haired woman said briskly. "We're going to have to get started on your costumes as soon as possible, especially the one for your solo number. I think a lavender dress would be beautiful for the Sea Queen." She shook her head. "But five weeks—I think they're crazy."

Danielle did as she was told, raising her arms and standing perfectly still as Mrs. Graves bustled around her with the tape measure.

The seamstress took Danielle's waist measurement twice. "Oh my," she said, shaking her head. "That can't be right." She consulted the small notebook in her hand and flipped back several pages. "Hmmm. According to this, you've gained two inches in the waist since last spring."

Danielle could feel her cheeks burning. She'd noticed that her jeans and skating dresses had become a bit more snug lately, but she hadn't paid much attention. Grandma Panati kept saying that she was "filling out."

"I think a dark color would be nice for you for the pairs number," Mrs. Graves said. "It will make you look slimmer."

"Maybe I should just wear white," Danielle joked to cover up her embarrassment, "so I can fade right into the ice."

Her friends laughed.

Mrs. Graves clucked her tongue as she took the rest of Danielle's measurements, and Danielle wanted to disappear in a puff of smoke. She couldn't be that fat, could she? After all, she'd just been picked to skate the part of the Sea Queen. Maybe the Sea Queen was supposed to be huge, Danielle thought suddenly. Maybe that was why she'd been chosen!

As soon as Mrs. Graves finished with Danielle and started measuring Nikki, Danielle found herself surrounded by other club members.

"You're so lucky, Danielle," Cheryl Slavin said, tossing back her long blond hair. "I bet Mrs. Graves will design you a great costume."

"Are you and Mr. Weiler going to choose new music for your program?" Diana asked. "We did last year for mine."

"I don't know," Danielle answered. "Probably."

"Just think of all the people who'll get to see you skate the solo," Martina Nemo put in. "There'll be reporters at the show and everything. Maybe you'll even get your picture in *Skating* magazine."

Danielle shrugged. "I kind of doubt it."

"Well, don't be too surprised if you get a lot of attention," Diana advised her. "I must have had at least three interviews over the phone last year, and then there was the article in the paper too." Diana squeezed her arm. "Congratulations, Danielle. This could be your first big break, you know?"

Danielle smiled. "I guess so." It felt nice to have so many people congratulating her. She couldn't remember Diana ever talking to her as if they were both on the same level—she was usually pretty snooty toward her and most of the other girls in the club.

Danielle spotted Tori on the other side of the dressing room. Her friend seemed to be concentrating very hard on getting every bit of dirty slush wiped off her skate blades with a rag. Mrs. Carsen was standing behind her, her lips pursed in an unpleasant expression. Danielle knew Tori was disappointed that her only solo was a short part in the rock-lobster number, and Danielle couldn't help feeling a little guilty about being chosen. After all, Tori was the more experienced skater.

But Mr. Weiler must think I'll be good, too, Danielle reminded herself, or he wouldn't have picked me. A shiver of excitement crept up her spine. How will it feel to be in the spotlight? she wondered.

That night Danielle's father insisted on taking the whole family out to dinner to celebrate. "We'll go to Giovanni's," he announced, throwing an arm around Danielle's shoulders. "Only the best for our skating princess."

"Daddy!" Danielle protested, blushing. "It's not that big a deal, really."

Mr. Panati gave her a look of mock indignation. "It most certainly is. Now, run upstairs and get ready."

Danielle did feel like a queen when they arrived at the restaurant. Mr. Panati had made reservations, and all of the waiters fussed over Danielle. The family had been going to Giovanni's ever since she could remember, and they knew almost everyone on the restaurant staff.

"Mario! The manicotti with a side of sausage, Danielle's favorite!" one of the waiters called into the kitchen before Danielle had even given him her order.

"Uh, I might have something else," Danielle said, biting her lip and frowning at the menu. Manicotti and sausage was awfully fattening. After being measured today, she wanted to watch her weight.

Grandma Panati leaned forward across the red-and-white-checked tablecloth. "What's the matter with manicotti?" she asked. "You love it here."

"I know, Grandma, but I kind of feel like eating something different," Danielle said. "I might have a salad instead."

Grandma Panati shook her head. "A salad's not enough. You need to keep your strength up, for training." She turned to the waiter, who was looking at them expectantly. "My granddaughter will have the manicotti, Sal, same as always."

"Grandma!" Danielle protested, but Grandma Panati waved her hand.

"And a side garden salad," her grandmother continued. "I'd like the chicken marsala."

"But Grandma, I'm trying not to eat so much," Danielle said, looking across the table at Nicholas. He was helping himself to his fourth piece of bread with two thick slabs of butter.

Grandma Panati laughed. "Nonsense. The manicotti is your very favorite, and this is a celebration. Now, eat!" She took the bread basket from Nicholas and set it down in front of Danielle.

Danielle hesitated. The bread smelled wonderful.

"I know what her problem is," Nicholas said. "She wants to be all thin and gorgeous for the show—right, Tubs?"

Danielle glared at him.

"Nicholas!" Mrs. Panati said. "That is quite enough. And please don't talk with your mouth full."

"Okay, Mom," Nicholas said. "I just have one more thing to say." He leaned across the table toward Danielle. "Jordan McShane."

"I don't know what you're talking about," Danielle replied.

"We heard the guys in Silver Blades talking about the show in the locker room. Jordan thought it was pretty cool that you got picked for the solo." Nicholas wiggled his eyebrows at Danielle.

Danielle wasn't sure whether her brother was making fun of her or not. He was probably just teasing her, as usual. But what if it was true? she asked herself. What if Jordan really did think it was cool? Maybe that meant he liked her. He *had* been really nice that afternoon at school.

She was saved from further teasing from Nicholas when some family friends came into the restaurant and took the table next to them. Soon more people were congratulating her and giving her hugs.

By the time a special dessert arrived for Danielle, a plate of pink, white, and green spumoni with a huge sparkler sputtering in the middle, she couldn't have been happier. She was going to be the Sea Queen in the Silver Blades Ice Spectacular, and Jordan McShane might actually think she was okay.

Danielle pushed Mrs. Graves and her nasty old measuring tape right out of her mind. I'll start my diet tomorrow, she promised herself, and dug up a huge spoonful of spumoni.

6

"Let's go, everyone!" Kathy yelled across the rink. "We don't have all day."

Reluctantly Danielle stepped out of the sound booth, where she'd been rewinding her cassette tape. It was Monday afternoon, time for the first group pairs rehearsal. She wasn't sure how it would go. The idea of skating with a boy was kind of exciting, but she'd never had a partner before. And learning to skate as a team took years of hard work. How would they ever manage to get a number ready for the show in just four weeks?

"This should be interesting," Jill said as she and Danielle skated toward the end of the rink. Danielle could tell that Kathy was getting annoyed. She was skating around in small circles, frowning down at the ice with her arms crossed. Kathy was a tough coach, and a former National championships competitor. Sometimes Danielle was glad Kathy wasn't her coach, though she knew she was a great one. Kathy was so demanding and tough on her skaters that, compared with her, Mr. Weiler seemed like a large, docile pussycat.

"Okay," Kathy said briskly when all of the pairs skaters had assembled. "We'll start off with a few basic moves. We won't bother with choreography until you've all gotten used to skating with a partner. Is everybody ready?"

No one answered, and Danielle glanced around at the others.

Tori stood scowling at Josh, her partner-to-be, clenching and unclenching her fists. Steve, who would be skating with Jill, was standing behind Kathy, shifting his feet. Mitchell was gazing at the American flag over the hockey scoreboard.

He doesn't look too thrilled about skating with me, Danielle thought. At least Nikki and Alex looked relaxed.

"All right," Kathy said briskly, "I want everyone to skate a few times around the rink with their partners, just to get used to each other."

Danielle took Mitchell's hand, but she had a hard time grasping it through his heavy mittens.

"This isn't going to work," Danielle said. "I can't even feel your hand. You've got to take those mittens off."

"Sorry," Mitchell said shyly. He stared at the ice

uncomfortably as he took off the woolly mittens and put them in the pocket of his warm-up jacket. How are we ever going to skate together if he won't even look at me? Danielle wondered.

As soon as they stood closer together, however, she realized that the two of them were well matched physically. But as they circled the rink, trying to match each other's speed and style, Danielle found herself being pulled and tugged. Every time she went one way, it seemed as though Mitchell was trying to go in a different direction.

Kathy skated up behind them. "Keep going, guys," she said encouragingly. "It takes time to get used to each other."

Then Kathy looked over her shoulder. "Get moving, you two," she told Tori and Josh. Josh, a fifth-grader, wasn't anywhere near as good a skater as Tori, Danielle knew. The only reason Tori had been paired with Josh was that she was short, and there weren't many boys in Silver Blades. It was obvious that the pair was having problems; Tori looked furious.

Jill and Steve weren't faring much better. They kept tripping all over each other as they circled the rink. Steve was a lot taller than Jill, but it seemed as if he was having a hard time keeping up with her.

The only pair that seemed to be working was Nikki and Alex. Alex, an eighth-grader at Kent, was a few inches taller than Nikki, but they had the same general build. Alex looked as though he might be able to lift Nikki easily. Unlike the other three boys, Alex's upper body was very developed from working out with weights a lot. Nikki and Alex were moving around the rink at the same pace, as if they were already used to each other's rhythms.

"Okay, girls, turn and start skating backward," Kathy called finally. "Boys, remember, you're watching out for your partners. The girls don't have eyes in the back of their heads, you know."

Danielle did a mohawk turn and suddenly came face-to-face with Mitchell. She grabbed hold of his bulky ski sweater instead of his shoulder and almost tripped.

Mitchell caught her just in time. "Nice move," he snapped. "You can relax now, you know—I've got you."

"Sorry," Danielle mumbled, feeling incredibly awkward. She glanced across the rink at her friends. Nikki and Alex moved smoothly together, skating faster and faster.

"Very nice, Nikki and Alex!" Kathy called. "Keep it up!"

At least someone knows how to do this pairs thing, Danielle thought, starting over with Mitchell. I sure don't!

Danielle pushed her way through the crowded school cafeteria on Friday and put down her tray at an empty table. Nikki and Jill were still in line getting their lunches. Danielle sighed as she sat down, her leg muscles aching.

Some of the shock and excitement of being picked to skate the solo in the Silver Blades show had definitely begun to fade. She felt exhausted, after only a few days of rehearsal for the ice show, and she wanted to work out even harder over the weekend.

Danielle picked up her carton of blueberry yogurt and opened her biology book. She'd been avoiding junk food all week and trying to eat as lightly as she could. Her goal was to lose ten pounds before the show. She had skipped breakfast again today, and she had a feeling that one measly carton of yogurt wasn't going to make a dent in her appetite.

"Hi, Danielle." Nikki placed her tray next to Danielle's. "Hitting the books again?"

Danielle gazed at Nikki's grilled-cheese sandwich and french fries. It looked a lot better than blueberry yogurt. Her mouth practically watered as she watched Nikki drag a french fry through a pool of ketchup and put it in her mouth. It's not fair, Danielle thought. Nikki eats all the time and she's as thin as a rail.

She focused once again on her textbook. "I need to do some extra studying," she told Nikki. "I haven't been concentrating too well on school lately."

Nikki smiled and popped another french fry into her mouth. "I can't imagine you not getting great grades," she said. "But you do have a lot to think about, with the show coming up and all."

Jill dropped into the chair across from Danielle. "Hi,

guys. Is that all you're eating?" she added in surprise, eyeing Danielle's yogurt.

Danielle shrugged. "I'm not that hungry," she lied.

"You've been having practically nothing at lunch for the last three days," Jill observed. "Are you sure you're getting enough to eat? During training it's important to eat a lot of carbohydrates."

"I'm just too excited to eat," Danielle explained, not wanting to hear a lecture on nutrition from Jill. "Nervous is more like it actually."

"Don't worry. I bet you'll do a great job in the show," Nikki said, smiling.

"Hey, that reminds me—I have some big news." Jill punctured the top of her juice carton with her straw.

"What?" Nikki and Danielle said together.

Jill looked smug. "I overheard Mrs. Bowen telling Tori's mom that a TV station, WSHP, is going to feature highlights from the Silver Blades Ice Spectacular on the evening news opening night. Isn't that great?"

"Wow," Nikki said.

"Yikes." Danielle gulped. Seneca Hills' local television station was coming to the arena? Television cameras would be filming her solo?

Jill leaned across the table. "Don't look now, but Jordan's sitting over there and he keeps looking at us. After what Nicholas told you the other night, I'm totally convinced he likes you."

"That is so cool," Nikki said. "He's really cute."

Danielle stared into her yogurt carton, too nervous to look over at Jordan. She wanted to believe that he liked her, but what if she was wrong? Maybe he was interested in Nikki, or Jill. They were much prettier than she, and they weren't so shy around boys.

She glanced at her watch, then stood up from the table. "I need to get in some last-minute cramming for my history test. I'll see you guys at the rink this afternoon."

Nikki looked at Jill and shrugged. "Okay. Good luck on your test."

"Thanks." Danielle headed toward the garbage with her empty yogurt container, being careful not to look in Jordan's direction. On her way she saw kids coming out of the lunch line with all different kinds of desserts on their trays: pie, packages of cream-filled cakes, cookies . . .

Danielle almost doubled back to buy a package of cookies to tuck in her purse for later. Maybe just a few cookies wouldn't wreck her diet, since she'd be skating later. Then she spotted Jordan at the end of the line. There was no way she wanted him to see her buying a snack, especially after Nicholas had called her Tubs in front of him.

She deposited the empty yogurt container in the trash can, then continued on to the library. Trying to diet was hard, but seeing Jordan had only increased her determination to lose weight before the ice show.

7

"**M**ore height, Danielle!" Mr. Weiler called. "Build up your speed for the takeoff and tuck hard in the air! Like this!" He snapped his arms in toward his chest.

On the ice on Friday afternoon Danielle was trying to push herself extra hard to learn the routine for the show—and burn off more calories. She'd been working with her coach on a new version of her old competition program to use for the show. Her old program had been designed to highlight her technical ability for the judges. Mr. Weiler had added some flashier jumps and footwork to jazz up her program so that it would appeal to an audience. He had also selected new music to go with her Sea Queen solo—a medley of songs from the movie *The Little Mermaid*.

Danielle was really eager to land her axel double-loop jump combination, which was the first big move in the Sea Queen program. But so far she'd been two-footing the landings every time. The axel double-loop combination was particularly difficult because the first jump, the axel, required a forward takeoff into a one-and-a-half-revolution turn in the air, and the second required a jump from the backward outside edge of her skate blade to complete two revolutions. The axel had to be landed cleanly, or the second jump would be impossible.

During her lesson with Mr. Weiler, Danielle had been going over the jump combination again and again. She was determined to land the double loop on one foot. Danielle began to circle the rink again. She gathered as much speed as she could, launched herself into the axel, and came down flatly on both skates.

Mr. Weiler threw up his hands in disgust. "That's enough for today, Danielle," he said as she skated over to the barrier. "You're still not getting enough height on those jumps."

Danielle frowned. That afternoon she had heard enough about height to last her a lifetime. She was trying as hard as she could, and for some reason it wasn't making any difference. She'd managed the jumps fine at the beginning of the week. Why did it always feel as if she was going "one step forward, two steps back" when it came to her skating? "I'm trying," she told Mr. Weiler, though she knew he didn't care much for excuses.

"I know it is frustrating," Mr. Weiler said. "But it is only through constant repetition that you will make this program as good as it must be. So we come back tomorrow and try again." He gave Danielle a small smile.

"Okay," Danielle said. At least Mr. Weiler was being understanding about it. Still, she kicked the barrier in frustration with her toepick as Mr. Weiler skated off to speak to Kathy, who was coaching Nikki on her layback spin. Nikki was leaning back gracefully as she spun, her arms above her head.

Danielle sighed. Mr. Weiler was probably going to tell Kathy how wonderful Nikki was—especially compared with Danielle. *Who am I kidding?* Danielle told herself as she hurried toward the locker room. *I'll never be able to pull off a solo performance. Why hadn't they chosen Tori or Nikki to perform the lead role?*

Danielle could hear the clock ticking loudly on the wall of the dressing room as she yanked at her skate laces. Her stomach was growling again, but she tried to ignore it. Once she lost some weight, she'd be able to get more height with her jumps. She should probably skip dinner. *Only three more weeks until the show,* she thought. *I hope I have enough time.*

On Saturday morning Danielle dragged herself down to the kitchen in her bulky plaid bathrobe, her hair in a messy jumble down her back. It was almost ten o'clock, and she still couldn't make herself wake up.

"Well, it's about time," Mr. Panati said as Danielle took her place at the breakfast table.

"I overslept," Danielle replied, stifling a yawn.

Mrs. Panati glanced at the clock. "At least you don't have to be at the rink until eleven-thirty today. Your father will drive you, honey, because I have a haircut appointment."

"What are you going to get, Mom?" Nicholas asked. He was manning the waffle iron at the counter. "How about a Mohawk haircut this time?"

Mrs. Panati laughed and shook her head. "I don't think so."

"Come on, you could dye it green," Nicholas urged. "Think how much Dad would like it."

"Just the regular cut, please," Mr. Panati said. "And you, pay attention to those waffles, or they'll burn."

"You went to bed at ten-thirty last night, Danielle," Grandma Panati said, frowning as Danielle got up to get a carton of skim milk from the refrigerator. "How can you still be tired?"

Danielle shrugged. "I don't know, Grandma. I guess I skated extra hard this week."

"Ah, the life of a future champion," Mr. Panati teased her. "Nicholas, don't forget to put on some extra waffles for your sister, the star."

"How many do you want?" Nicholas asked Danielle with a sigh. "There's bacon too."

"I'm not having any waffles," Danielle said, putting a box of corn flakes on the table. She sat down and poured a small amount into a bowl, then added milk.

"What do you mean, you're not having any?" Grandma Panati asked. "You've hardly been eating anything at all for the last few days. That little bowl of cereal isn't going to fill you up."

Here comes another argument with Grandma, Danielle thought. I hope she isn't going to make me eat again. But before she could say anything, the doorbell rang.

"I wonder who that is," Mrs. Panati said, looking up from the newspaper.

"It's Jordan," Nicholas said, heading over to the door. "We're going to a football game at the high school."

Danielle felt the spoonful of corn flakes stick to the roof of her mouth. Jordan—at her house?

"I don't think I know Jordan," Grandma Panati said. "Does he go to your school?"

"He plays hockey with Nicholas," Danielle told her. How on earth was she going to get out of the kitchen? She couldn't let Jordan see her looking like this!

Nicholas opened the door. "Hi, Jordan," he said, giving him a clap on the back. "Come on in and meet the family."

I can't believe this, Danielle thought miserably. The guy I've had a major crush on since the sixth grade is going to see me in my oldest bathrobe and fuzzy blue slippers.

"Hey, everybody, this is Jordan McShane," Nicholas announced, bringing him into the kitchen. He winked at Danielle behind Jordan's back.

Danielle wished she were invisible, but there was no getting out of the situation now. "Oh, hi, Jordan," she said brightly, pulling her bathrobe tighter around her waist.

If Jordan thought she looked ridiculous in her pajamas, he didn't show it. "Hi, Danielle," he said with a grin, running a hand through his dark hair. "Hi, everybody," he added to the rest of the family around the table.

"Jordan, won't you sit down and have some waffles?" Mrs. Panati asked. "Nicholas is our chef this morning."

"Danielle, aren't you going to be late for the rink?" Grandma Panati said. "Maybe you should go up and get ready." She gave Danielle a meaningful look and nodded toward the door.

"Excuse me, I'll be right back," she said, jumping up from the table. Thank you, Grandma! Danielle added in her head. You must be a mind reader.

She hurried out of the kitchen and took the stairs two at a time. She had to get dressed and make herself look halfway presentable before Jordan left.

Danielle threw open her closet door and gazed inside. Her best skating dresses were hanging on the left, just above the shelves jammed with sweaters and tights, but she didn't feel like wearing a dress today. There was another group pairs rehearsal that afternoon, and she'd probably be taking a lot of spills.

She finally decided on a shiny black unitard with a hot-pink stripe and a matching pink-and-black Scunci in her hair. She quickly brushed her hair into a soft ponytail and pulled on her black high-top sneakers.

Much better, she told herself, surveying her reflection in the mirror above her dresser. The unitard seemed to make her look a lot thinner.

She picked up her skating bag and rushed back downstairs. She was glad to see Jordan still sitting at the kitchen table. She smiled faintly at him as she sat down. Was it her imagination, or had his face lit up when she came into the room?

"So, uh, who's playing today?" she asked him. "I mean, the football game."

"Oh, it's Grandview High against Frontier," Jordan said, nodding. "It should be good."

"Don't you guys have practice?" she asked.

"Not today," said Nicholas. "At least *some* of us get our weekends off."

"Hey, I didn't make up the schedule," Danielle protested.

Jordan cleared his throat. "We'll probably go over to the rink anyway after the game to practice shots at the hockey session."

Really? What time? Danielle wanted to ask. She stopped herself. Not only would she sound dumb, but she'd never hear the end of it from Nicholas.

"Come on, Dani—time to go." Her father stood in the doorway, jangling the car keys in his hand.

Danielle stood up and grabbed her skating bag. "See you guys later," she said.

"Yeah, maybe I'll see you at the rink," Jordan said.

For a second, he almost looked like he did want to see me later, Danielle thought as she slid into the car seat. The whole way to the rink Danielle couldn't stop thinking about the way Jordan's expression had changed when she came into the kitchen.

"**W**e'll begin with something easy today," Kathy said at the start of Saturday's pairs practice. "Girls, take your places in front of your partner."

Everyone did as they were told. Danielle couldn't help noticing that Mitchell seemed very nervous. He was probably afraid she was going to crash into him again. She wished he would talk more. He was so shy that he barely said anything to her on the ice. Meanwhile Tori and Josh argued nonstop.

"I never said that!" Tori cried.

"Yes, you did!" Josh replied angrily. "I heard you. You said you should be skating with a *real* skater. As if I'm not a real skater—I mean, at least I can jump without—"

"Okay, you two," Kathy said, putting her hands on

her hips. "I'm not going to put up with any of this nonsense. The show is less than three weeks away. If you guys want to argue all the time and not learn the routine and then make fools out of yourselves in the show, that's fine with me. But just remember, you'll be letting down everyone else in this number. Am I making myself understood?"

"Yes," Tori mumbled. Josh nodded and poked at an ice chip with his skate blade.

"Good." Kathy looked around at the four pairs of skaters. "Rule number one of pairs skating is that both partners have to work at getting along. You need to be able to trust each other, because some of the moves you'll be doing could be dangerous if you're not careful. That said, let's get moving."

Kathy skated to the center of the ice. "We're going to learn pair spins. Both skaters will have to work together and skate as a unit. It's a little different from the side-by-side jumps we've done before."

Danielle felt the color rise to her cheeks. When she and Mitchell had tried side-by-side axels at the last practice, they couldn't manage to land at exactly the same time. Kathy said that either Danielle had to increase the speed she rotated in the air or Mitchell had to slow down his one-and-a-half-rotation jump. Danielle had never known doing a jump next to someone could be so difficult. She had always been told that her axel was excellent when she performed it alone.

Kathy motioned for the four pairs to spread out and find places on the empty ice. "The pair sitspin is approached by backward crossovers in the clockwise direction," she instructed.

Sliding her right foot repeatedly across the front of her left foot, Danielle desperately wished she and Mitchell could get their backward crossovers in the same rhythm. She watched Nikki and Alex's backward crossovers with envy. Their bodies moved in time with each other. It seemed as if each knew exactly what the other was thinking. Danielle sighed. She had absolutely no idea what was going through Mitchell's mind.

"Keep in time. One, two, one, two," counted Kathy. "Tori, you're skating too fast!"

Tori reacted by glaring at Josh. Danielle almost laughed. Wide-eyed, Josh looked petrified of Tori.

"Now, entering the spin, both skaters step toward each other," said Kathy. "You should end up facing each other while spinning in the sitspin position."

Danielle hesitated a second, watching Nikki and Alex do it. She couldn't get over how well they skated together. Both of them were spinning rapidly on their left feet, in the classic sitspin sitting position.

Danielle gave Mitchell a nod to start the spin.

"Jill! Steve! Get closer!" Kathy yelled, breaking Danielle's concentration. Jill and Steve were spinning about six feet from each other, while Nikki and Alex seemed to have only inches separating them.

Danielle and Mitchell swung into the spin at the same time. Danielle tried to control the speed of her spin. She made eye contact with Mitchell, hoping this would make them skate as a unit. But shy Mitchell quickly cast his eyes down to the ice, throwing off both their rhythms.

Kathy clapped her hands. "This is *pairs,* folks. Work *together.* Watch Nikki and Alex's spin. And then everyone do it again, and again, and again!"

After calling the practice to an end, Kathy signaled for the group to meet her in the center of the rink. "We're making some progress—not much, but at least there's hope." She smiled faintly. "Nikki and Alex, you both did a terrific job today. Have you ever thought about skating pairs in competition? Because I think you should. Ordinarily I wouldn't suggest that you rush into a decision like this," Kathy went on, "but the Regional competition is coming up soon, and very few pairs have registered so far. It would be a perfect opportunity for you two. We could begin serious training right after the show."

Neither Alex nor Nikki said anything right away. They both looked as if they were in a complete state of shock.

"I have a feeling you'll want some time to think about this," Kathy said. "You can give me an answer next week sometime."

"Okay, sure," Nikki replied.

Alex nodded. "I guess I could think about it." He turned to Nikki. "Maybe we would have a pretty good chance of winning."

"Well, you two think about it, talk about it—let me

know how it goes," Kathy said. "I'll see you at our next practice." She skated away, leaving the four pairs standing on the ice.

"I'll see you later," Alex said to Nikki before he skated off with the rest of the boys.

"Wow," Jill said, raising her eyebrow. "Kathy was serious. She really thinks you and Alex make a good pair."

"What do you think, Nikki? Do you want to give up singles skating?" asked Tori.

"I don't know." Nikki looked confused. "All I've ever done is practice for singles competitions. What do you guys think?"

Danielle was quiet as she listened to her friends discuss the issue. The truth was, she felt envious of Nikki. While Danielle was constantly being criticized, Nikki was skating as if she'd been with a partner her whole life. Danielle wanted to be happy for her friend, but she was too worried about her own skating problems. Danielle had never felt so competitive.

What's happening to me? she wondered. Is it the pressure? Maybe being a top skater isn't what I want after all.

9

Danielle stood at the edge of the rink, waiting for her music to start. The bleachers were filled with fans—so many that it was standing room only. As she struck her opening pose, she caught sight of Jordan sitting in the front row, right next to Mr. Weiler. She felt as if she'd been waiting forever for her tape to play. She glanced over at the sound booth. Suddenly some marching music that sounded like a Fourth of July parade blasted out of the speakers.

Danielle looked at Mr. Weiler, terrified. "This isn't my music!" she whispered fiercely. Mr. Weiler only nodded, signaling that she should proceed.

Danielle pushed off tentatively with one skate. She tried to coordinate her footwork to the music, but it was too fast, and she got all out of sequence. She was afraid to look at Mr. Weiler for help. She didn't want Jordan to think that she didn't know what she was doing. Somehow she had to make it through her solo.

She prepared for her first big jump, a double salchow. Just as she lifted into the air, the music changed again—into a slow, haunting melody. I can't jump to this! Danielle thought as she crashed onto the ice.

Danielle woke up with a start. For a second she stared at the clock radio beside her bed. Then she realized she had only been having a bad dream.

She started to pull the covers up over her head, then threw them back again. "Stop it!" she told herself. "It was only a dream. That's not going to happen."

The clock radio on Danielle's nightstand said eight-fifty. Even though it was Sunday, the only day of the week that Silver Blades didn't practice, Danielle was determined to get on the ice. Her dream had made one thing clear: She was nervous about her program because she needed to work on it. She'd lost too much precious time yesterday during that worthless pairs rehearsal.

She padded down the hall in her bare feet and knocked on her parents' bedroom door. "Dad!" she called.

"Danielle?" a sleepy voice replied.

"Dad, could you drive me to the rink this morning?"

Mr. Panati opened the door. "It's Sunday," he said with a yawn. "Your day off, remember?"

Danielle shook her head. "I'd really like to go anyway, if you wouldn't mind taking me."

"All right," Mr. Panati said with a sigh. "Give me half an hour."

"Thanks, Dad," Danielle said. She ran back to her room and hurriedly pulled on an oversized green sweater and black leggings. The leggings seemed a bit looser, but it was hard to tell for sure, since they were so stretchy anyway. Maybe she was finally beginning to lose weight.

Danielle hurried across the hall to the bathroom and stepped on the scale. She was two whole pounds lighter, even with all her clothes on! Danielle threw her arms over her head. The diet was working!

Danielle went downstairs to the kitchen and poured a glass of orange juice for herself while she waited for her father. She almost had some leftover coffeecake, too, but she stopped herself just in time. If she had even a tiny bite of anything sweet, she might go overboard and eat everything in sight.

Fortunately her grandmother was still asleep, so no one noticed that she was skipping breakfast again. Danielle took a plate from the cupboard and smeared a little strawberry jam on it. Now it looked as if she'd had some toast, and her grandmother would stay off her back.

When Mr. Panati finally dropped Danielle off at the arena at nine-thirty, she saw with dismay that both of the rinks were already being used for public sessions.

There were dozens of people on the ice—families with kids, many of them clutching the barrier, teenage girls, boys on speed skates, and elderly couples waltzing slowly along the end of the rink.

Danielle walked across the hall to the exercise room, which fortunately was open. She placed her skates on the floor, in the corner, and closed the door behind her. At least she could have some privacy.

She stretched out for a while at the barre, then moved on to a few floor exercises, checking her positions carefully in the mirror. She definitely looked thinner, she noticed. In fact she even felt lighter. She could hardly wait to get on the ice and try some jumps.

There was a light knock on the door, and Jill poked her head inside the studio. "Want some company?" she asked.

"Jill!" Danielle said in surprise. "What are you doing here?"

"Same as you," Jill replied. "I haven't been getting much practice in, between show rehearsals and running after my little brothers. Toby told me I'd find you in here. Are you ready to hit the ice yet?"

"Sure," Danielle replied, picking up her sweater and skates. "But I have to warn you, both of the rinks are jammed."

"I kind of figured they would be," Jill said with a sigh. "I guess it's worth a try, though."

They walked out to the bleachers and sat down so that they could put on their skates. Danielle could practically lace her skates with her eyes closed, she'd done it so many times. But she was using a new pair of skates today, and they were still very stiff. She quickly threaded the laces through each hole.

"Hey, Danielle—what's with your hands?" asked Jill suddenly.

Danielle stopped and looked at her hands. "What do you mean? Do I have a wart or something?"

"No—they're shaking," Jill said. "Let me see. Hold out your hands."

Danielle extended her arms. "I don't see anything."

"Come on, Dani. All of your fingers are quivering," Jill stated. "Are you sick? Maybe you have the flu."

"No, I am definitely not sick," Danielle said, starting to lace her skates again.

"Maybe you're not eating enough or something," Jill said. "My mom gets shaky when she's really hungry. That's probably it. You probably haven't been eating enough, with those little yogurts for lunch."

Danielle shrugged. "I've been eating plenty. I'm just on a diet, that's all."

Jill gave her a skeptical look. "I don't know, Dani. There's dieting, and then there's starving yourself."

"I know what I'm doing," Danielle said. "I just want to take off a few pounds before the show." She stood up and pulled the cuffs of her leggings down over the top of her skates.

"Well, I personally don't think you need to lose any weight," Jill said.

"Then you're the only one," Danielle said. "Everyone around here's been commenting on it. I'm sick of it. So I'm doing something about it."

Jill shrugged. "Whatever. Just don't overdo it."

"I won't," Danielle said, thinking privately, It's not as if Jill knows anything about dieting. She's never had to go on a diet and she probably never will.

Danielle stood beside the barrier looking at the crowded rink. She was about to step onto the ice when three people collided right in front of her.

"Yikes," Jill said. "Maybe skating this session isn't such a good idea. We're never going to get any serious practicing done." She turned to Danielle. "I've got a great idea. Let's go to the mall this afternoon and put up posters for the ice show. We can call Tori and Nikki and see if they can come too."

Danielle hesitated. "I don't know . . . I really need the workout."

"Come on," Jill urged her. "You can't even jump in this crowd."

"Okay," Danielle agreed finally. She'd just have to work extra hard tomorrow.

At the mall the four members of Silver Blades lingered near the central fountain, trying to decide where to go next. They'd just finished putting up the posters for the ice show in about a dozen stores at the mall.

"Well, I could use a new pair of jeans," Tori said. "Let's go to Canady's."

Jill nodded, and Nikki turned to Danielle. "Sounds

good to me," Danielle said, even though she had absolutely no intention of trying on clothes. Not until she had lost some more weight.

But when the girls emerged from the store, Tori and Nikki carrying brightly colored bags, Danielle felt a little sorry for herself. She'd broken down and tried on a pair of stretch jeans, but they hadn't stretched at all on her. In fact they'd been just plain tight.

She stopped short as the smell of melting cheese, tomato sauce, and pepperoni began wafting through the air. A nearby stand was selling pizza and calzones. No, she told herself. Keep going.

Suddenly Jill pointed toward a movie marquee halfway down the mall. "Hey, look, what's playing! *Monster from the Lost Planet*! Want to go?"

Tori glanced at her watch. "What time did we say we'd meet your mom?"

"Five-thirty," Jill replied. "We'll just make it."

Danielle looked at the movie poster, which showed a gruesome, fire-breathing monster devouring an amusement park. She hated movies like that, and she really didn't want to spend the rest of her allowance on it.

"Uh, would you guys mind very much if I wandered around the mall for a while instead?" Danielle asked. "I need to buy a present for my grandma's birthday, and—"

"Forget the movie, then," Jill said quickly. "We'll help you pick something out."

"It's okay, really," Danielle assured her friends. "Enjoy the movie. You've been dying to see it, Jill."

"Well, all right, if you're sure," Nikki said. "We'll meet you outside the video arcade afterward."

As soon as her friends disappeared into the theater, Danielle continued on her way down the mall. After a bit of searching, she bought a pretty embroidered teapot cover for her grandmother at one of the gift carts in the middle of the floor. Then she stopped to gaze at the miniature carousel as it spun gleeful children around and around. Finally she came to Arnie's Video Arcade.

Danielle stepped into the arcade and waited for her eyes to adjust to the darkness. She drifted to the back, where a group of noisy kids was gathered around a virtual-reality game. She tried to watch for a while, but the game was so crowded that she couldn't see a thing. Finally she turned to the next machine, where a dark-haired boy was engrossed in a video hockey game.

Danielle looked again. She couldn't believe it. She was standing right next to Jordan.

Suddenly Jordan turned toward her and grinned. "I just won a free game," he said.

"Not bad," Danielle replied, trying to sound casual.

Jordan laughed. "Think you can do better?"

"Maybe," Danielle answered with a smile.

"You're on," Jordan said.

For the next few minutes the two of them battled it out in video hockey. Danielle put up a good fight, but

Jordan scored higher on every screen. "I play this one a lot," he admitted sheepishly.

To even the score, Danielle challenged him to Space Avengers and easily beat him four games to one.

"Not bad, for a figure skater," Jordan said.

Danielle grinned and punched him lightly on the arm. "Don't be too upset. Figure skaters are just more coordinated than hockey players."

They tried a few more machines, until they had both run out of quarters. Now what? Danielle wondered. Things had been going so well, now what would they talk about?

"How's the team doing?" Danielle asked. "I mean, I hear about it from Nicholas, but he only tells me how he does."

"Pretty good. That new guy, Kyle, is fantastic," Jordan said, shaking his head. "I bet he'll play in the pros someday."

"Really?" asked Danielle. Kyle Dorset was new in Seneca Hills, and he and Nikki had gone on a couple of dates, including the fall dance last month. "That's amazing."

"How are the rehearsals for the ice show going?" Jordan asked. "I heard you have a big solo."

"Yeah." Danielle nodded.

"I can't imagine what it would be like, skating all by yourself in front of people," Jordan said. "I'm so used to being on the team, six guys out there at once. Don't you get nervous?"

"Actually, I've never had a solo before," Danielle

admitted. "This is my first big role—and yeah, I'm really nervous. It's all I can think about."

"So this is like the big time, right? I mean, it'll be just you, skating to music, the way they do in the Olympics?" asked Jordan.

Danielle couldn't believe he was interested in hearing about her skating. "It's similar to what they call the long program in competition," she told him. "It lasts three minutes, and you have to use the whole ice surface—the whole rink. *And* you have to do as many hard jumps as you can. I'm glad this isn't a competition—just an exhibition. Mr. Weiler still has me doing lots of jumps, though, and they're—sorry," she said, blushing. "I'm probably boring you to death."

"No, you're not," Jordan said quickly. "The show sounds really cool. I'll be cheering for you on opening night."

"Thanks," Danielle said, her heart pounding harder. He was going to see her skate! She wasn't sure how to feel—excited or petrified.

Jordan nodded and swiveled back and forth in his chair in front of the machine. The two of them continued talking for a long time—about figure skating, hockey, school, music, everything! Danielle even told Jordan that she was a fan of old black-and-white movies. She couldn't believe how easy it was to talk to him.

About fifteen minutes later Nikki, Tori, and Jill came into the arcade, looking worried.

"Danielle! We've been searching all over for you,"

Nikki said. "You were supposed to meet us outside of this place, remember? Jill's mom is waiting for us."

Danielle jumped off her stool. "Sorry, guys," she said. "I totally lost track of the time."

"I wonder why," Tori teased.

Danielle quickly said good-bye to Jordan, and the three girls hurried toward the parking lot.

"So, now we know why you didn't want to go to the movie!" Nikki said.

"I didn't know he was going to be in there," Danielle protested, laughing.

"So, what were you guys talking about that was so fascinating?" Jill asked. "Me, I hope?"

As they slid into the backseat of Mrs. Wong's car, Danielle hit Jill playfully on the leg. "No, we were talking about my solo actually. Guess what? He said he's coming to opening night!"

Nikki turned around from the front seat. "You're kidding! He must really like you, then."

"Yeah—but did you tell him he'd have to sit through our pairs number first? 'The Skating Sailors Who Can't Skate'?" Jill joked.

"More like 'The Stumbling Sailors'!" Danielle said, and laughed. She was so glad she'd decided to go along with Jill and come to the mall. Now she didn't feel worried about the show, or about losing weight. And was it her fault Jordan just happened to be at the mall too?

Later that night Danielle tried to do some home-work, but she couldn't concentrate. She was just too tired, and the words kept blurring on the page of her textbook. At this rate she'd never be able to keep her grades up. Besides, she was absolutely ravenous.

Maybe Jill's right, she thought. Maybe I should be eating a little more.

Danielle swung her legs off her bed and headed down to the kitchen. What she needed right now was a burst of sugar to give her enough energy to study.

She peered inside the refrigerator. Cold cuts, leftover pot roast, orange juice, lettuce—nothing too exciting there, she thought, closing the door.

Then she spotted the seven-layer chocolate cake her grandmother had baked that morning. It was practi-cally calling to her from its glass-enclosed pedestal.

Danielle took a knife from the drawer and cut her-self a tiny piece. The frosting was so delicious that she polished off another extra-small slice. What's the harm of just one more? she asked herself as she lopped off a little more. But before she knew it, she had worked her way through almost half of the cake.

10

"**D**anielle, I understand you're skating a solo in the Silver Blades Ice Spectacular in three weeks," said Ms. Nguyen, Danielle's humanities teacher, on Monday morning.

Danielle nodded, and felt a faint blush creeping up her neck.

"That's terrific! I heard that part of the opening night of the show is going to be shown on the late news." The teacher turned to the rest of the class and smiled. "Isn't that wonderful?"

Danielle looked down at her desk and forced herself to smile. It *would* be wonderful, she thought, if I could stick to my diet. How could she have eaten so much the night before? After all those weeks of dieting she'd blown it in just one night. Now she would never lose any weight.

"Congratulations, Danielle," Beth Moore told her. "That's great!"

"I knew you skated all the time, but I didn't know you were actually any *good*," Doug Kirk teased her.

"Like, can I have your autograph?" Cecily Thorne smiled at Danielle.

Everyone was being really nice, but Danielle wished they would all leave her alone. She didn't want to hear about how great she was and that the ice show would actually be on TV. It made her even more nervous. How would she ever be able to perform when everyone she knew, everyone in Seneca Hills, was watching? She'd be totally paralyzed with nerves. And when a skater froze up, it was all over—she might as well not skate at all, because she was sure to fall.

Grow up, a different voice inside Danielle commanded. If you want to be a skater, you're going to have to learn how to handle the pressure.

At the rink Thursday afternoon Danielle sat on the boards, taking a break with Nikki.

"I really haven't decided yet about pairs," Nikki said. "I've been thinking about it nonstop. What do you think, Danielle?"

Danielle shook her head. "That's a tough one," she said. "Has Kathy said anything else to you about it?"

Nikki sighed. "No. We're supposed to get together and talk about it this afternoon."

"Well, maybe you should make a list or something. You know, pairs versus singles, pros and cons. Or maybe Kathy would let you train for both."

Just then Mr. Weiler skated over to the barrier. "This is no time for you to be gabbing with your friends, Danielle," he scolded. "You have plenty of work to do on your program. In fact I'd like you to run through the whole thing right now. With the music, please."

Danielle jumped off the barrier and went over to flip on her cassette at the sound booth.

Then she positioned herself in the center of the ice, with her head bowed and her arms crossed gracefully in front of her.

Suddenly her new music, the medley from *The Little Mermaid*, blared from the loudspeaker. On the fourth beat Danielle slowly raised her arms over her head and pushed off with her toepick. She lifted her right leg off the ice, gliding forward on her left, and concentrated on arching her back and raising her right leg into a dramatic spiral that showed off her flexibility.

The music's tempo quickly increased, and Danielle began an intricate footwork pattern. She tried to check her turns sharply so the footwork looked crisp and precise. Then she switched directions with backward crossovers and headed diagonally across the rink. She focused on her first jump combination, a delayed axel right into a double flip jump. She had only landed her double flip for the first time last month. Danielle realized midway through the axel that her timing was off. She managed to hold on to the landing, but barely made it into the double flip with enough power.

The music continued to pick up pace, and Danielle pushed herself to keep in time with it. After several quick backward crossovers, she glanced over her right shoulder, reached her right arm back, and dug her right toepick into the ice. Then, in a split second, Danielle looked forward, brought her right arm forward and her left arm back, and lifted into her double Lutz jump. She rotated counterclockwise twice in the air. Danielle could feel how low her jump was and knew she had overrotated her upper body on the lift-off.

After the double Lutz she immediately went into her hardest spin combination—a back camel jump sitspin. Then the music became more melodic, and Danielle began the transition into the slower part of her program. This section had the softer-edge jumps, like the double salchow and the double loop, as well as her graceful layback spin. Danielle particularly liked showing off her artistry and balletlike choreography in this part of the program.

Finally, in the last thirty seconds of her performance, the music turned increasingly faster. Danielle could hear the heavy pant of her own breathing. She completed the strenuous double salchow–double loop combination, two toe-touching split jumps, and a flying camel spin. She finished the program with a dramatic spread-eagle glide as the music faded away into silence.

But even before the music had ended, Danielle knew what her coach was going to say: The footwork had gone fairly well, and she'd done some nice spins, but the jumps were much too low—still.

Mr. Weiler set his coffee mug on the barrier. "Not bad, Danielle," he said. "But those jumps . . ." His voice trailed away.

Danielle scraped at some ice shavings with her skate blade, unable to meet her coach's eyes. If she couldn't turn in a decent performance during a routine practice, how was she ever going to get through her program in the show?

"I'd like to see your program again," the coach said with a sigh. "And this time I'm going to have Kathy take a look at it."

Danielle's heart skipped a beat. What did Kathy have to do with anything? Were they looking at her program to see if it was good enough for the show?

"Let's go, Danielle," Mr. Weiler said. "We don't have all afternoon. And don't leave out that double Lutz jump this time," he called as she skated away. Then he beckoned to Kathy, who had just finished giving Nikki a lesson.

Danielle signaled for her music and took her position on the ice. Maybe Kathy would be able to give her some tips on her jumps, she thought. Maybe Mr. Weiler had run out of ideas and he needed Kathy's help.

She ran through her program once again, trying even harder than usual to land all of her jumps cleanly. Unfortunately the knowledge that both Kathy and Mr. Weiler were watching wasn't helping her concentration much. Preparing for the tricky double Lutz, Danielle did some backward crossovers and positioned herself on a backward outside edge. Then she placed her right leg back, jumped into the air off her toepick—and got absolutely zero height on her jump. She barely completed the rotations in time before she landed shakily.

Danielle finished out the program, but even her final split jumps, which she usually did well, were unusually low. She skated back to the barrier, afraid to look at Mr. Weiler or Kathy.

The two coaches were huddled together, talking. Neither one looked happy. They're going to throw me out of the show, Danielle realized. I was right—I'm not good enough after all.

Kathy cleared her throat. "Danielle, I'd like you to come with me. We need to talk."

11

Danielle followed Kathy off the ice, her hands shaking as she reached for her skate guards on the barrier. Was she really going to be taken out of the show?

"Let's go into my office," Kathy said.

It's even worse than I thought, Danielle realized. It wasn't very often that members of Silver Blades had to speak with a coach alone.

The walls of Kathy's office were covered with skating photos and posters. Many of the pictures were of Kathy during her competitive days. The others had been given to her by former students and friends from the international skating world, including several medalists from the last Olympics.

"Sit down, please, Danielle," Kathy told her.

Danielle nervously clenched and unclenched her

hands in her lap as Kathy rummaged through some videocassettes on a shelf behind her desk.

Across the hall Mr. Weiler's door was open. The whole room was cluttered with papers, old skating posters and magazines, and music tapes. Where was he anyway? Danielle wondered. Shouldn't he be here too? After all, he was her coach.

"Aha!" Kathy said, pulling out one of tapes and slipping it into the VCR beside her desk.

"What's that?" Danielle asked, frowning.

"You'll see in just a moment," Kathy said, fiddling with the control buttons. "But first," she added, turning back to Danielle, "I want to let you know that we're making some changes in the show."

Here it comes, Danielle thought, her heart sinking. She's going to tell me I'm through as the Sea Queen.

"Mr. Weiler and I have decided to take you out of the team precision number, since those rehearsals haven't started yet. That way you'll have more time to practice for your solo, since you're already skating in the group pairs number."

Danielle let out her breath in a deep sigh. She hadn't even realized she was holding it.

"I hope you aren't too disappointed," Kathy said. "I know that skating in the precision number is a tradition for the girls in Silver Blades."

"Oh, I don't mind that much," Danielle assured her. It would have been fun, of course, but the important thing was that she was still getting to skate the solo. This might give her the extra practice time she needed.

"Good." Kathy nodded and turned on the small television monitor. "Mr. Weiler asked me to make this tape when you were running through your program the other day," she said. "I thought you should see it."

Danielle leaned forward in her chair as the tape began. She could hear her program music playing faintly as her tiny image launched into the opening move, a graceful spiral down the center of the ice. Suddenly there was a crash of cymbals, and she struck a dramatic pose before beginning an intricate series of footwork. Then she built more speed with backward crossover steps, to prepare for her delayed axel jump. Stepping forward onto her left skate, she threw herself into the air, trying briefly to delay her rotation for greater effect, but the jump was way too low. Danielle cringed as she watched herself come down on two feet.

As the tape continued to play, Danielle noticed, she wasn't getting height on *any* of her jumps, not even the easy ones. She looked sluggish on the footwork, even in the fastest part of the program, and the dance moves that Mr. Weiler had added to jazz up her routine looked awkward. Her program was terrible, all right, but the worst part was her appearance. She looked absolutely huge on the ice—like an elephant in a short skating skirt.

Kathy must have read her mind, because she quickly said, "Don't forget, Danielle, the camera always adds about ten pounds."

Danielle sat for a moment, stunned. Then she jumped up. "You and Mr. Weiler did this on purpose!" she practically shouted. "You wanted to show me how awful I looked so I'd lose weight before the show. That's why I'm not landing my jumps."

"Wait a minute, Danielle," Kathy said sharply, snapping off the monitor. "Your coach and I had absolutely no intention of showing you this tape for any reason other than letting you see how your choreography might be improved."

Danielle barely heard her. She was furious with Kathy and even more furious with Mr. Weiler. She couldn't believe he had gotten another coach to do his dirty work.

"I know all anyone cares about around here is how heavy I am and how I'm going to ruin the show," Danielle continued angrily. "Don't worry—I'll be thin by then. I won't embarrass you on TV!"

With that she whirled around and stormed out of Kathy's office. She pushed through the swinging bathroom door, then stopped in her tracks. Jill, Melinda Daly, and Diana Mitchell were leaning against the sinks, talking. Danielle started to back out of the bathroom.

"Danielle!" Jill called. "Come back!"

It was too late. The other girls had already seen her, and they knew she was crying. Jill hurried over and put an arm around Danielle.

"What's wrong?" she asked.

"Nothing." Danielle sniffed. She didn't want to talk about it in front of Melinda and Diana. Especially Diana. She always seemed so perfect.

But Diana said, "Come on, Danielle. You can tell us."

"I'm just worried about how I'm going to look for the show," Danielle said. "Kathy took me into her office and showed me this videotape—"

Jill rolled her eyes. "Dani, you always worry, and you always do well," she said. "You think you bombed an algebra test and then you get a hundred on it. You tell me you can't write papers and you always get A's. Then I hand in something I think is great—and I get a C-minus." She shook her head. "I swear, it's disgusting!"

Danielle shook her head. "This is different," she said. "You should have seen me in that video. I looked like a fat pig! Kathy just didn't have the nerve to come out and say it."

"Danielle, get real," said Diana. "Have you ever known Kathy to be afraid to say anything? I have a feeling she wanted to talk about your skating, not your weight."

"Diana's right," said Jill. "You're overreacting."

"Listen, Danielle," Diana said. "If you're going to be a competitive skater, you've got to be tougher. How can you improve if you can't take criticism?"

"And a lot of us have to watch our weight," Melinda put in. "It's just part of being a skater."

"I've been there," said Diana. "I've always had to be careful about my weight."

Danielle was surprised. "You? But you're so—" She wanted to say "perfect."

"Of course me," said Diana. "But it's not the end of the world. The important thing is to learn how to eat and not to go overboard with dieting. A skater's got to be healthy."

Jill said, "It doesn't matter how skinny you are if you can't make your jumps."

Danielle nodded. She could see their point. But they hadn't seen her on the videotape.

"We'd better get back out on the ice," Melinda said. "Feel better, Danielle?"

"Yes," Danielle said. "Thanks, guys. I'll be out in a few minutes."

The other girls left the bathroom. Danielle ran cold water over a paper towel at the sink and held it to her eyes. They still looked a bit puffy, but maybe no one would notice. Diana was right. She needed to be a whole lot tougher if she was going to be a competitive skater.

She was going to have to apologize to Kathy too. She really hadn't meant to blow up like that. Kathy was only trying to help.

Danielle squared her shoulders and left the bathroom. She went back to Kathy's office and was about to go in when she heard Kathy talking to somebody else.

"Well, Nikki? Have you made a decision yet?"

"Not exactly," Danielle heard Nikki reply. "I was wondering whether I might be able to compete in pairs and still skate singles too."

Kathy sighed and said, "Let me be perfectly honest

with you, Nikki. You've done a fantastic job so far as a member of Silver Blades. You've worked very hard, and your skating has already improved quite a bit. There's no telling how far you could go in a singles career."

Danielle took a few steps closer. She didn't mean to eavesdrop, but this was pretty interesting. At least Kathy thought someone in Silver Blades deserved some praise.

"Then why do you think I should skate pairs?" Nikki asked.

"Well," Kathy said, "there are many, many girls out there, just like you, who want to be Olympic champions. They have talent and drive, they receive top coaching, and they put in endless hours of ice time. But how many of those girls do you think can win Olympic or World championships?"

"Not many, I guess," Nikki said.

"Now, I'm not saying that you wouldn't make it to the top as a singles skater," Kathy went on. "But I think your chances would be a hundred times better if you and Alex competed as a pair. For one thing, the number of pairs skaters is far smaller, and for another, the two of you are extremely well matched. I think it's worth a try."

"Okay," Nikki said. "I guess we could try it for a while, and see what happens."

"I've talked about it with Alex, and he's interested," Kathy went on. "But I think you're right—we'll consider the next few weeks a trial period. Work together, see how it goes. Now, you asked me whether you could compete in both singles and pairs. The truth is, it can be done, but it will take an extraordinary amount of dedication and hard work on your part. You're already spending most of your waking hours on the ice, but it's up to you. Why don't we go for it? After all, strong singles skaters make better pairs skaters. And if it doesn't work out, it doesn't work out."

Danielle gazed up at the picture on the door to Kathy's office. It showed a man and a woman dressed in dramatic black-and-red costumes, performing a star lift. The woman was nearly horizontal in the air as her partner held her with only one hand. They made it look effortless. Maybe someday Nikki and Alex would be that good.

"Okay," Nikki said. "I'll do it!"

"That's great," said Kathy. "I'm excited for you."

Danielle loudly cleared her throat and knocked on the door. "Sorry, I couldn't help overhearing. Go for it, Nikki. I think you and Alex make a great team."

"Thanks." Nikki smiled.

"Uh . . . can I talk to Kathy for a second? Alone?" asked Danielle.

"Sure. I'll see you in the locker room." Nikki left and Danielle sat down in the chair opposite Kathy's desk.

"I'm sorry about what I said earlier," Danielle said. "I guess—I've just been kind of nervous. I didn't mean to yell."

Kathy nodded. "That's okay. Not that I want you to keep doing it, but I understand. There's a lot of strain on you when you're rehearsing for a big show—I remember what that feels like. The important thing to remember, Danielle, is that we all want the same thing. A fantastic ice show. If Coach Weiler or I say anything to you, it's because we want to help."

Danielle nodded. "I know. And I promise, I'll work on my jumps even harder this week. I think I can see what I'm doing wrong."

"Good. That's all I wanted to show you on the tape. You need to think about your program as a whole—make the whole thing flow together. Right now it's simply in several parts," Kathy said.

Danielle nodded. "Okay. Thanks for the help." She stood up to leave.

She was halfway out the door when Kathy said, "And Danielle? Don't forget—to be a great skater, you need to stay motivated. If you need any help, just ask."

"Thanks," she told Kathy. "See you tomorrow morning."

Danielle knew her program still needed plenty of work—the videotape had made that obvious. But she was convinced that as soon as she lost more weight, the jumps would be easier, the dance steps would flow more smoothly, and there would be nothing she couldn't do.

12

The next Monday morning Danielle dragged her tightest jeans out of her closet and threw them on the bed.

This is the moment of truth, she thought. So far, according to the bathroom scale, she'd lost six whole pounds. Now it was time to see whether she was really getting any thinner or whether the scale was lying. She'd read somewhere in one of her mother's magazines that quick, early weight loss was mostly water, not fat, but she didn't care. Six pounds were six pounds.

Danielle stepped into the jeans and yanked on the zipper. It zoomed upward like magic. "Yes!" she said aloud, doing a little victory dance. "It's working!"

She stepped into her moccasins and hurried downstairs, jumping to the floor from the third-to-the-last step. She'd be landing her jumps on the ice in no time!

But dieting was getting harder and harder, Danielle reminded herself as she walked quickly past the kitchen. The most difficult part was skipping meals without her family noticing. It was easy enough at school, where she had a yogurt or an apple for lunch, but getting away without food at home was another story.

Now she got up even earlier than usual every morning so that no one could see what she was—or wasn't—having for breakfast. Dinner was the hardest meal to skip. For one thing she was always starving when she came in from the rink. It was torture sitting at the dinner table, pushing the delicious-smelling food around with her fork as Nicholas stuffed his face.

Sometimes she got away with saying she'd eaten at the rink, which didn't make her mother very happy. Last night Danielle had told everyone she'd microwave leftovers after she finished her homework. She knew she couldn't keep up all of this meal skipping for long of course, but she was sure she could keep her family fooled at least until the show was over.

Danielle was breaking a piece of bread into crumbs to leave on a plate, as usual, when she heard her grandmother say, "Are you making some breadcrumbs for the birds, Danielle?"

She whirled around, with half a piece of whole wheat bread in her hand. "Oh, uh, hi, Grandma. I didn't know you were up."

Grandma Panati looked at her suspiciously. "Just what are you doing with that bread?"

"Oh, I was . . . just breaking it up into pieces so I could dip it in jam," Danielle said. "You know how much I love that." She smiled nervously. That was a lousy excuse, she thought. I've never eaten that before in my life.

"Is that right?" Grandma Panati muttered. "Are you sure you don't want some cereal? I could make some oatmeal."

Danielle glanced at her watch. "I'd love some, but Dad's going to be down any minute to take me to practice."

"Then let me make you a sandwich to eat later," Grandma Panati said. "Some nice roast beef, a little cheese—"

"No, Grandma," Danielle said, irritated. Why was her grandmother always trying to make her eat? It was hard enough staying on a diet without people trying to force food on you all the time. "I mean, no, thank you."

Grandma Panati shrugged. "You look a little pale this morning. Are you feeling all right?"

Danielle heaved a sigh of relief when her mother walked into the kitchen. Now she could get away from her grandmother's prying questions. "I feel *fine*, Grandma," she said. "I feel terrific."

And I've lost six pounds already! she reminded herself as she grabbed her skates from the hall closet.

Wednesday afternoon Danielle couldn't wait for the pairs rehearsal to be over. Kathy had called an extra group pairs practice. Danielle was a bit disappointed that her lesson was canceled for the day—after last week's talk with Kathy she was determined to do her best—but the pairs number had been such a disaster so far that she couldn't really protest.

The only problem was that the practice was dragging on and on, as Kathy made them all go through a few basic lifts. Danielle and Mitchell were getting absolutely nowhere.

"You're too heavy," Mitchell complained, setting Danielle down before he'd lifted her above the top of his skates. "I can't do it."

Danielle glared at him. "Try it again," she said, between clenched teeth.

Kathy clapped her hands. "One, two, three, lift! Very nice, Nikki and Alex. Keep holding on, Jill and Steve. Mitchell—oh, dear."

Danielle felt her partner drop her like a sack of cement. It was no use, she thought miserably.

But Kathy didn't seem very upset. Instead she called the group together again. "Nikki and Alex, you're making incredible progress," she said. "Jill and Steve, you're getting there. Maybe you can work a bit on synchronizing your footwork. Jill, you're going to have to bring your jumps down a bit to match Steve's."

Then she turned to Danielle and Mitchell. "I think you two should do a bit of off-ice work," she said. "Let's go to the weight room and see what we can do to get those lifts going."

Danielle's heart sank. The last thing she felt like doing right now was working out with weights. She was absolutely exhausted.

She and Mitchell followed Kathy off the ice to the weight room. It was hot and stuffy inside. A few club members were already working on the machines or standing in front of the mirror with free weights.

"I'll bet you two didn't know that the girl usually does more work on a lift than her partner," Kathy said.

Danielle and Mitchell just looked at each other.

"That's right," Kathy went on. "It's actually up to the girl to push herself into the lift and hold herself in position. The boy ends up looking like some kind of superhero, but his partner is really working just as hard, if not harder."

"I can't lift Danielle at all," Mitchell said, avoiding her eyes. "She's not helping, and she's almost as big as me."

"Nonsense," Kathy said briskly.

Danielle smiled gratefully.

"How do you suppose Tai Babilonia and Randy Gardner, the American pair who skated in the Olympics a while back, did lifts after Tai ended up growing taller than Randy?" asked Kathy. "They managed, and so can you. I happen to know that

Danielle is very strong." She nodded toward one of the weight machines behind her. "Danielle, why don't you show Mitchell just how strong you are?"

Danielle walked over to the huge black machine. She reached for the bar and brought it down slowly as she took her place on the narrow seat.

"Okay, Danielle," Kathy said cheerfully, adjusting the pins that controlled the amount of weight she would have to push. "Let's start you off nice and easy."

Danielle started to lift her arms—then stopped. She felt as if she had absolutely no energy. She strained to press the weights, but she couldn't budge them. "I—I can't," she said, letting out her breath.

"Try it again," Kathy instructed. "Come on, I know you can do it—I barely put any weight on there."

Danielle pushed as hard as she could. The weights moved a few inches up, and she released the bar. The weights crashed down with a loud bang.

Kathy frowned. "Danielle, are you feeling all right? You normally lift a lot more than that. You know, you don't look very well either."

"I'm fine!" Danielle told her. But even as she spoke, the room was beginning to get sort of fuzzy.

"That's enough for today," Kathy said firmly. "I shouldn't have tried to push you so hard after practice like this. Besides, you need to save your strength to work on your own program, as well as the pairs number. I want you to go straight home and get some rest. We'll try this again tomorrow."

Half an hour later Danielle dropped her bag at the foot of the stairs and headed up to her bedroom. "Good night," she told everyone. The rest of the family was sitting at the dining room table.

"Danielle, aren't you eating tonight?" her mother said, looking worried. "Are you feeling sick, dear?"

"No," Danielle said, grasping the banister tightly. She was afraid she might fall back down the stairs if she didn't hold on to something. "I'm just really tired."

"It's all this training for the show," Mr. Panati said, shaking his head. "I want you to take it easy, Danielle. I think you're overdoing it."

"Maybe she'd feel better if she had some meat loaf and mashed potatoes," Grandma Panati said.

For the first time since Danielle had started dieting, the idea of eating a whole dinner wasn't even tempting. She was just too tired. "Maybe later," she mumbled, and made her way up the rest of the stairs.

She lay in bed for what seemed like hours, but as tired as she was, she couldn't seem to fall asleep. What was wrong with her?

Suddenly there was a knock at the door. "Come in," Danielle called.

Grandma Panati came into the room, carrying a tray. "Here you are, Danielle," she said, placing the tray on the bedside table. "I've brought you a nice, hot meal. And I'm going to sit right here until you've eaten it," she added.

"But, Grandma—"

"No *buts*," her grandmother said, sitting on the edge of Danielle's bed. "Start eating."

Danielle knew better than to argue with her grandmother. She took a few mouthfuls, and Grandma Panati looked pleased. It wasn't that she wanted to hurt her feelings, she thought as she forced another bite to her mouth, but she really wasn't that hungry. Her stomach seemed to have shrunk.

"Danielle, you know you can always talk to your grandma," Grandma Panati said, leaning forward. "If there's anything bothering you, dear, you don't have to keep it all inside. Are you sure there's nothing wrong?"

Danielle hesitated. Should she tell her grandmother how nervous she was about the show and how badly she wanted to lose weight so that she could jump higher, skate faster, and look thin and graceful in her Sea Queen costume?

No, she decided. This was something she'd have to deal with all by herself. Besides, her grandmother didn't believe in diets. She would only make her eat.

"I'm fine, Grandma," she lied. "There's nothing wrong."

13

Thursday morning Danielle woke up feeling a little better, until she realized she had slept through her morning practice. Why hadn't anyone called her?

She sighed and got out of bed. There was no point in rushing now, she thought. At this rate she'd be lucky if she made it to school.

As she passed the hall mirror on her way to the stairs, Danielle was startled by the sight of her reflection. She looked pale and drawn, and there were huge bags under eyes, even though she had slept for nearly twelve hours. At least I look thinner, Danielle told herself tiredly.

When she entered the kitchen, her mother was sitting at the counter drinking a cup of coffee.

"Good morning, honey," Mrs. Panati said. "How are you feeling?"

"Better," Danielle replied. "But I missed practice."

Her mother nodded. "I wanted you to get some extra sleep this morning. In fact, I think you should stay home from school."

"But Mom—" Danielle began to protest.

Mrs. Panati held up one hand. "Danielle, you are not going to school today, and you are not going to the rink. We were all very worried about you last night."

"Oh, all right," Danielle said with a sigh. Actually she was glad she'd have a chance to get more sleep, but she hated the idea of missing a whole day of skating. Opening night was only nine days away!

Danielle slept all morning. Her mom had decided to work at home today because Danielle wasn't feeling well. She came up once to tell Danielle she was going to drive Grandma Panati to the dentist. She tried to get Danielle to have some lunch, but Danielle said she felt nauseous, which was almost the truth. She still didn't feel like eating at all.

Around one o'clock the phone rang, and Danielle padded across the hall to her parents' room to answer it. "Hello?" she said into the receiver.

"Danielle, this is Mr. Weiler," her coach said. "Is everything all right? Kathy told me you weren't feeling very well last night, and when you didn't show up at the rink this morning . . ."

Just then Danielle spotted the morning newspaper

on her parents' bed. There was a front-page article about the upcoming Silver Blades Ice Spectacular and an interview with Mrs. Bowen, the club president. Immediately the butterflies began to dance in her stomach.

"Uh—I'm better now," she told her coach quickly. "I'll ask my mom if I can come to practice this afternoon," she added quickly.

"It's a shame that you had to miss the club sessions today," Mr. Weiler said, "but I don't want you pushing yourself too hard. Stay home and rest, and I'll see you tomorrow at the special practice session. It's more important that you attend that."

"All right," Danielle said. There was no use pretending she'd make it to the rink today. She felt awful. Besides, it was sort of a relief to be away from the pressures of the rink for a day. "Thanks, Mr. Weiler."

"Go back to bed," Mr. Weiler said. "And eat some chicken soup or something, yes?"

Danielle laughed. "Okay." She couldn't believe how nice Mr. Weiler was being to her. Maybe he agreed with her mother—she needed some rest. After today, I'll probably skate a lot better, she thought as she trudged back up to her room.

Later that night Danielle was making a feeble attempt at doing some homework when the phone rang.

"Danielle!" Nicholas called. "It's for you. Some guy," he added with a grin as he handed her the phone.

Danielle glared at him and took the receiver. For a second she thought it must be Mr. Weiler calling back to tell her he'd decided to take her out of the solo since she wasn't feeling well. "Uh, hello?" she said nervously, waving at her brother to leave the room.

"Danielle, it's Jordan," a familiar voice said. "How are you doing?"

"I'm okay," Danielle replied, her heart pounding. What did he want? He sounded nervous too.

"I was, uh, looking for you at school today," he said. "Nicholas told me you weren't feeling too well."

"I'm fine now," Danielle said. "I was just a little tired, that's all."

"Great," Jordan said. "I mean, I'm glad you're not sick or anything. Listen, I was wondering if you might want to go to the movies with me tomorrow night at the mall, if you're feeling okay. *Monster from the Lost Planet* is playing." The last few words came out in a rush.

Danielle couldn't believe it. Jordan was actually asking her out! But what was she going to tell him? Tomorrow was the extra-long Friday-night practice session. She'd planned to do some serious work on her solo then, especially after she'd missed both practices today. And she had a whole hour's lesson scheduled with Mr. Weiler. She couldn't just skip the practice.

But Jordan will never ask you out again, said a voice

inside her head. And it's not as though you've been skating well anyway. Will missing one more practice really make a difference?

Before Danielle could think about it for one more minute, she blurted out her response. "The movie sounds great," she told Jordan. "What time should I be ready?"

"A date?" Mrs. Panati looked as if she had just heard that there were aliens living next door instead of the Petersons. "You want to go on a date?"

"Mom, you're acting like it's the craziest thing you're ever heard of," Danielle protested.

"Well, I'm just—surprised," Mrs. Panati said. "I didn't know you and Jordan were . . . friends." She drummed her fingers against the kitchen table. "What about skating practice? Isn't there a special session tomorrow night?"

"Mr. Weiler told me to take the night off," Danielle quickly lied. "He doesn't want me to push myself."

"Maybe a night off from skating is a good idea," Mrs. Panati mused aloud. "You've been working so hard." She looked Danielle in the eyes. "Jordan is a very nice boy, but it is your first date. I'll have to discuss this with your father first."

"Mom! Please?" Danielle asked.

Mrs. Panati smiled. "Don't worry. I can be very persuasive."

"Danielle, where is your head today?" Mr. Weiler asked at Friday afternoon's practice session. "You seem to be, what is the expression . . . going through the motions."

Danielle blushed. "I'm sorry. I guess I'm still a little sick." She looked down. The truth was she couldn't think about anything except how guilty she felt about missing tonight's practice.

"I have a suggestion. Why don't you leave practice a little early today and take a nap before tonight's special session," Mr. Weiler said. "I want you to be able to focus. Have you been getting enough sleep?"

"Sure," Danielle said. "I mean—I think so." She looked down, embarrassed. Mr. Weiler was telling her to take a nap and rest up for that night's practice, when she wasn't even planning on showing up.

"I think I'll stay," she murmured. "I want to work on my routine some more."

Later, in the locker room, Danielle wanted to tell Nikki, Jill, and Tori about her date, but she couldn't bring herself to do it. They'd be furious with her and tell her she was making the wrong decision—even if it meant missing the date with Jordan.

I'll tell them later, Danielle decided as she packed her skates into her skate bag. After the show.

"Danielle, my mom's going to drive me and Jill over for the practice tonight," Nikki said, slinging her bag over her shoulder. "Should we pick you up too?"

"Oh, uh—no," Danielle said, flustered. "We—I think we're going out to dinner. My parents will just drop me off afterward."

"Where are you going to dinner?" Jill asked.

Danielle thought quickly. "I'm not sure actually. My mom said it was a surprise." She shrugged. I can't believe I'm lying to my friends too! "But thanks for asking, Nikki." She smiled at Nikki and Jill on their way out of the locker room. For a second she thought she saw Jill giving her a suspicious look. Danielle felt as if her friend could see right through her.

"**I**'ll have the Scooperama," Jordan said. "With chocolate chip, rocky road, and Pralines n' Cream. Extra hot fudge, please."

"And what would you like?" The waiter turned toward her.

"Oh, uh . . . a diet cola," Danielle said. "And a glass of water."

"That's all you're going to have?" asked Jordan. "Don't you want even a cone or anything? My treat."

Danielle shook her head. "No, thanks." She took a straw from the container on the small marble table at Super Sundaes in the mall and started drawing on the table with it. She wasn't sure she was going to have anything to say to Jordan, now that the movie was over. He'd been so nice, paying for her ticket and holding her hand during the scary parts. She liked him even more than before—but that made her even more nervous. What if he didn't feel the same way about her?

She couldn't stop thinking about how disappointed Mr. Weiler had sounded when she called to tell him she couldn't make it to practice that night. She'd told him she was just feeling too worn out to come—that she was suffering a relapse from Thursday. "But I'll be all better tomorrow," she had told him. "I guarantee it. I just need a good night's sleep." Now here she was, going out for ice cream after watching the movie with Jordan. She felt incredibly guilty for lying again. But every time she looked at Jordan, she told herself she had done the right thing.

"That movie was pretty bad, huh?" Jordan asked as the waiter set down his huge sundae on the table. Jordan picked up a spoon and dug into the ice cream.

"Well . . . yeah," Danielle said, and they both laughed. "The special effects were cool, though," she added after a minute, slowly sipping her soda.

"You don't like horror movies, do you?" Jordan asked.

Danielle smiled. "How could you tell?"

Jordan pointed to his arm, which had a small red mark on it. "This is where you dug your nails in when that green stuff came out of that dead guy's eyes."

"I'm sorry!" Danielle said. "I didn't know I was doing that."

"Just remind me to wear my hockey pads on our next date," Jordan said, and smiled.

Danielle could hardly believe her ears. *Our next date?* Things were going even better than she expected. She was about to ask Jordan about a hockey game he had on Saturday when she heard a familiar laugh coming from the mall's side entrance, near the door, followed by some loud shrieks and giggles.

Jill! she thought. She glanced in that direction. Her friend was walking toward the ice-cream parlor with her mother and her younger brothers and sisters.

Danielle slinked down in the booth and waited till Jill and her family were seated across the restaurant.

Then she gave an exaggerated glance at her watch. "Oh, no! We're supposed to meet my parents outside now. We'd better go."

"But—" Jordan looked down at his half-eaten sundae.

"They really hate it when I'm late," Danielle said, standing up and turning up the collar of her jeans jacket. Jordan tossed a few dollars on the table and stood up. "Let's go," Danielle said, pulling on Jordan's arm. She practically dragged him out of the ice-cream parlor.

Danielle felt bad about rushing their date, but there was no way she was going to let Jill find out she wasn't really sick after all.

"Did you have fun?" Mrs. Panati asked when Danielle and Jordan slid into the backseat of the Volvo.

"It was great," Danielle said with a nervous glance at Jordan.

"Yeah," Jordan said, and smiled. "It was."

By the time they'd finished dropping off Jordan, then picking up Nicholas at a friend's across town, it was after ten. When they walked in the door, Danielle noticed that the light on the answering machine was flashing. Danielle pressed the Rewind button. "Hi, Dani, this is Jill. I just got home. Can you call me tonight when you get in? It's really, really important. Thanks."

Danielle's heart sank. Jill must have seen her at the ice-cream place.

"I wonder what that's all about. I've never heard Jill sound so serious," Mrs. Panati said, pouring herself a glass of seltzer water.

Danielle didn't answer her mother as she walked up the stairs to her room. Instead she was thinking, I know what it's about—Jill wants to yell at me for skipping practice.

The worst part was, Danielle knew she deserved to hear every word.

When Danielle entered the locker room the next morning, her friends were already there. She hadn't called Jill back last night, and now she avoided her friend's eyes.

"You must have been really sick last night," Nikki said sympathetically. "Did you have a relapse?"

"Uh, not exactly," Danielle said, glancing nervously at Jill. She was surprised that Jill hadn't already told Nikki and Tori about seeing Danielle at the mall last night.

"We all figured you wouldn't miss another practice so close to opening night unless you were practically on your deathbed," Tori said. "Well, don't worry—there's great news. We're off the hook on the group pairs number."

"Nikki and Alex are going to skate it without the rest of us," Jill explained. "Kathy thought it might be too much for you, after being sick and all. That's what I wanted to tell you last night." She gave Danielle a knowing look, and Danielle felt like crawling under the locker room bench.

She couldn't stand lying to her friends any longer. "You guys, there's something I have to tell you. I wasn't sick," Danielle confessed in a rush, looking down at the rubber-matted floor. "I went to the movies with Jordan."

Tori's eyes widened. "You did what?" she cried.

"I can't believe it," Nikki said, shaking her head. "Your parents actually let you go?" She sounded shocked. "What if Mr. Weiler finds out?"

Danielle sighed. "I know I shouldn't have done it. I was just so excited that Jordan actually asked me out, and I guess I got carried away. . . ." Her voice trailed off.

Her friends were silent for a moment. Then Jill said, "Dani, can I ask you something?"

Danielle nodded.

"Why are you doing this?" asked Jill.

"Doing what?" Danielle was confused.

"I don't know. It just seems like you're trying to mess up this solo on purpose or something," Jill said. "Why else would you skip practice? You're not eating, you don't even seem to be trying—"

"I'm trying!" Danielle protested, stung by her best friend's words. "I'm trying as hard as I can."

"Danielle has been practicing nonstop," Nikki chimed in. "It just hasn't come together yet, but it will."

"I think so too," Tori said.

Jill shook her head. "I've known Dani for two years, and she's never skipped a practice. *Never*. Now, when it's her first big break, all of a sudden she thinks a date is more important. I don't get it."

"Of course you don't get it," Danielle said angrily. "You don't know what I've been through. Ever since I got this solo, everyone's been on my case about my skating and how fat I am. It hasn't been any fun at all. Then, finally, one good thing happened to me— Jordan asked me out. I knew I shouldn't go, but—I don't know, I can't explain it. I was afraid I'd never get another chance."

"So you'd rather have one date than the biggest

chance to skate you've ever had?" Jill countered.

"Look, we'd better get going—practice has already started," Tori said, pulling at Jill's sleeve. The two of them walked out of the locker room, and Danielle just stared after them. How could Jill be so mean? She didn't understand what it was like, to be afraid of skating in front of a big crowd.

"Don't let what Jill said upset you," Nikki said. "She's a little angry, but she'll get over it."

Danielle shook her head. "It's not that, Nikki." She was about to confide in her friend about all the doubts she'd been having and how afraid she was of failing, when Kathy stuck her head into the locker room.

"Danielle! Mr. Weiler's waiting for you!"

Danielle sighed loudly and followed Nikki out and down to the rink. Maybe she could talk to Nikki about it later. At least Nikki seemed to care—all Jill wanted to do was criticize her.

As Danielle skated toward Mr. Weiler for her lesson, she noticed that he was looking at her strangely. Now what? she thought. Had Jill already told him that she hadn't been sick last night?

"Danielle, before we start, I'm worried about something," he said, frowning. "You've been so sick lately. I'm afraid you've lost some weight."

Danielle's heart nearly stopped in her chest. Wasn't that the whole point? "Maybe I have. I wanted to lose some pounds so that I could improve on my jumps."

"Well . . . it may help," Mr. Weiler said. "But you don't look very healthy."

Lately, whatever I do is wrong! Danielle thought in anger. First I'm too heavy, and then I'm too thin! "I'm fine, really," she told her coach. "I slept a lot last night."

"All right, then," Mr. Weiler said. "Let's work on some spins today for a change of pace. How about a flying camel?"

Danielle nodded and began some backward cross-over steps to build up speed. For the flying camel, she would have to start on a forward outside edge, then whip her free leg around and jump into a fast spin on her other foot. The more speed and height she could get on the jump, the faster she would spin.

Setting her arms carefully, she paused on her backward inside edge, then stepped forward onto her left leg. Her skate wobbled a bit as she leaped into the air, and Danielle wasn't sure where the ice was beneath her. Suddenly she felt incredibly dizzy as the ice rose to meet her, and everything went black.

15

The next thing Danielle knew, she was lying on a cot in the arena's first-aid room, surrounded by people. Toby Mullen was bending over her, rubbing her wrists, and Mr. Weiler and Kathy were standing behind him, looking worried. Mrs. Bowen was there, too, waving a tiny package of smelling salts under Danielle's nose.

"Wh-what happened?" Danielle asked. Her head was throbbing, and the smell of the ammonia made her feel sick to her stomach.

"You had a nasty fall," Kathy told her, sounding unusually gentle. "But you're going to be fine."

"Do you think she should go to the hospital?" Nikki asked Mr. Weiler.

"I don't need to go to the hospital," Danielle started to protest, but Mr. Weiler shook his head.

"We don't know how hard you hit your head when you fell on that flying camel spin," he told her, "and any injuries like this need to be checked out, just in case. You wouldn't want to be skating around with a concussion."

The paramedics arrived a few minutes later, and Danielle saw her friends standing in the doorway, white-faced, as she was rolled onto a stretcher.

Jill rushed over to her as the paramedics carried her out the door toward the waiting ambulance. "Dani, I'm sorry about what I said before. I only wanted to help you—honest," she said.

Danielle smiled weakly. "I know. And anyway, I deserved it."

"I'll come to the hospital and see you, okay?" Jill called as Danielle was placed in the back of the ambulance.

At the Seneca Hills Clinic an hour later Danielle lay on another cot in a curtained-off room, waiting for the doctor to come back. When he finally pushed back the curtain, Danielle saw that he was smiling.

"You're going to be just fine," he told her. Then he turned to Danielle's parents, who were hovering anxiously next to her bed. "We're going to send her home, but I'd like you to see that she takes it easy for the next day or two. I'm fairly sure there's no concussion, but you'll need to keep an eye on her."

"Can I skate?" Danielle asked anxiously. "I'm supposed to be in a show on Saturday night."

"We'll see," the doctor replied, consulting his clipboard. "That's a week away—you should be fully recovered by then. Even by Wednesday. However, I do have some questions for you, Danielle. We think you may simply have fainted. Can you tell me what you've eaten over the last few days?"

Danielle glanced at her parents, then told the doctor all the food she could remember. It wasn't much, she knew. Her mother and father looked shocked as she listed the yogurts she'd eaten for lunch, how she'd skipped breakfast, and eaten only vegetables for dinner for the past week and a half.

"Dani, when I said you should eat healthier food, I didn't mean you had to cut out everything!" Mrs. Panati said, concerned.

"I'm surprised this didn't happen earlier," her father said. "How did you manage on so little food?"

Danielle shrugged. "I just wanted to skate well for the show. Mr. Weiler said I wasn't getting enough height on my jumps, and that if I wanted to, I'd have to lose some weight."

The doctor tapped his clipboard. "Unfortunately crash dieting like this is a fairly common practice for some athletes, especially skaters, dancers, and gymnasts. Even boxers, wrestlers, and jockeys sometimes go overboard to keep their weight down. But from now on, Danielle, if you want to lose weight, you should diet only under a doctor's supervision, and not for a while. You don't need to starve yourself to be healthy. From now on—especially until the show—I want you eating several small, healthy meals a day until you regain your strength."

"We'll see that she does, Doctor," Mrs. Panati said, looking at Danielle. "We're sorry we didn't catch on before this."

"Oh, crash dieters are pretty good at hiding their eating patterns," the doctor said. "I'm sure Danielle went to some effort to keep you from knowing what she was doing."

Danielle thought of the jam she'd smeared on plates and the crumbs she'd left, and how she'd pushed her food around to make it look as if she'd eaten. She had been hiding a lot from everyone. She lay back on the cot, thinking as her parents talked with the doctor for a few more minutes.

When the doctor had gone, Danielle's father helped her to her feet. She glanced at both of her parents. "I'm sorry, Mom and Dad. I know I've been doing some dumb things. I guess I've just been feeling a lot of pressure about the ice show. I've never skated a solo before, and I'm so afraid of . . ." Danielle's eyes filled with tears.

Her mother reached for her hand. "You always put so much pressure on yourself, honey. You don't have to be perfect all the time, you know."

"That's right," said her father. "Skating should be something that you enjoy, Dani. We don't want you to feel miserable about it."

"Thanks, guys," she said softly.

"Danielle, if you don't want to skate the solo—" Mrs. Panati began.

"No, Mom, I do," Danielle quickly interrupted. "I've

been waiting for a chance like this for two years. I really want to perform that solo."

"Then you'll have to follow doctor's orders, young lady," said Mr. Panati. "That means three square meals a day."

"Don't worry, Dad," Danielle assured him. "I have every intention of eating whatever Grandma puts on my plate!"

"I'm so glad you're all right," Jill said that night when she, Tori, and Nikki stopped by the Panatis' to see Danielle.

"Yeah, there's no way we can have the ice show without you," Tori said. "Unless of course Nancy Kerrigan flies in for the weekend."

"Yeah, right!" Danielle laughed. "I'm sure we're in the same league."

"You could be," Nikki said. "Eventually anyway. I heard Mr. Weiler talking to Kathy this afternoon, and he said he was relieved to hear you were okay."

"Then they gave us a talk on nutrition, about the proper way to eat while you're training," Tori said.

"Like it helps you now, right?" Jill teased. She smiled at Danielle and picked at the fringe on a pillow on her bed. "You know, Dani, I really didn't mean to yell at you this morning. I just couldn't believe you'd pick Jordan over Silver Blades—over us."

Danielle smiled at her friend. "Skipping practice was

a pretty stupid idea," she admitted. "Don't worry—I'm not going to do that again."

"Hey, I didn't say you couldn't see the guy!" Jill said, laughing.

"Yeah, it's not like you can't ever date," Nikki said. "I mean, I go out with Kyle once a week usually." She shrugged. "It'd be fun to see him more, but there just isn't time."

"At least you guys are allowed to date," Tori said. "My mother won't let me go out with anyone until I'm fifteen." She shook her head. "It's so embarrassing."

"But what if I tell Jordan I can't go out with him?" asked Danielle. "He'll probably just ask someone else."

"I doubt it!" Jill said. "Didn't you just say he called you twice today to see if you were okay?"

Danielle blushed. "Yeah . . . but—"

"Yeah, but nothing," Jill said. "He likes you, Dani. A lot."

"Just promise us one thing. Make a date with him for *after* the ice show, okay?" Tori asked.

Danielle nodded. "He's coming to opening night, he said."

"I can't wait for opening night," Nikki said. "I'm so nervous about skating with Alex."

"You guys look great together," Danielle reassured her.

"It's going to be a terrific show," Jill said. "But before you start skating again on Wednesday, you'd better eat whatever your parents tell you to. We don't want you keeling over again."

"Yeah, the Sea Queen's not supposed to conk out on the ice," Tori said. "Unless, if you want, we could ask Mr. Weiler to change your routine—you know, make it a little more exciting."

Everyone started laughing. "No, that's okay," Danielle said with a grin. "I like it just fine the way it is."

16

On Friday, the opening night of the Silver Blades Ice Spectacular, Danielle stood nervously backstage, wearing her lavender skating costume. She would be going on for her solo in just a few minutes.

She gingerly touched her hair a few times, to make sure the bobby pins holding the heavily sprayed bun were still in place and her tiara wasn't going to fall off. So far, so good.

Danielle knew she was lucky to have recovered quickly enough to skate in the first performance of the show. Her whole family, especially her grandmother, had been fussing over her for the last few days, and once she'd started eating balanced meals, she'd begun to feel much better. She'd even gotten on the ice several times to go through her program before the show.

She'd had plenty of good wishes from everyone, too, especially her friends and Jordan. Tori, Jill, and Nikki came over during the week to make decorations for the show and keep her posted on all the last-minute preparations, and Jordan had shown up at the door with a cluster of balloons.

The junior members' group number was just ending, and the rest of the girls in Silver Blades were preparing to go on for the team precision number.

"Good luck, Danielle," Diana said as she took her place behind the curtain.

"You'll do great, Dani," Tori told her, and Jill and Nikki both gave her victory signs. The Caribbean music for the precision number was already filling the arena.

Danielle waved to her friends as they skated out, and peered through a small hole in the curtain. When the house lights came up again, the members of Silver Blades stood in one long line, their arms around each other's shoulders. Slowly they made their way down the ice, high-kicking in unison and smiling to the audience.

"Are you ready, Danielle?" Kathy asked, coming up behind her. "I know you're going to do a great job."

"Thanks," Danielle said. "I hope so."

"Just try to forget about all the people out there," Kathy said. "Pretend you're in a regular practice or on a lesson with Mr. Weiler."

Danielle nodded, but inside she was wondering how she could possibly forget the audience. Practically everyone she knew was in the audience, including her family, her classmates, and Jordan. And, she reminded herself, there were TV cameras posted at the other end of the rink.

She shook that thought out of her mind and leaned forward to watch the other skaters again. Right now they were skating in a rapidly spinning line, rotating around the two tallest girls in the middle. It was a formation often used in professional ice shows, in which skaters tried to catch the end of the line, one by one.

Suddenly one of the girls on the end let go by mistake, and the line went on without her. In a few moments the other skaters, unable to stop because they were moving so fast, would plow straight into her!

As Danielle watched in amazement, Tori burst out from the side and grabbed the panicking girl by the hand, pulling her to safety just in time. The crowd clapped and whistled.

"All right, Tori!" Danielle shouted as her friend gave a little wave to the audience. Mrs. Carsen beamed with pride from her seat in the bleachers.

The precision number ended a few minutes later, and the arena lights began to dim. Danielle stepped back from the curtain as the skaters made their way backstage.

"Nikki, let's go!" Mrs. Bowen called frantically. "You're going to have to change fast. You and Alex are on next!" Then she turned to one of the younger girls and said, "Megan, skate over to the sound booth and tell Mr. Ortega to stall. He's announcing the numbers too quickly."

Nikki changed into her pairs outfit in record time and joined Alex behind the curtain. Danielle thought he looked as nervous as she herself felt, but Nikki seemed cool as a cucumber. The two of them skated out onto the ice to a loud round of applause.

The lights dimmed, and a bright white spotlight highlighted Nikki and Alex posed on the ice, in shimmering blue-and-silver sailor costumes, ready to begin their program. As the opening melody of Debussy's *La Mer* filled the arena, Alex gave Nikki a reassuring smile, grasped her hand, and they began to skate.

Danielle held her breath as they prepared for their first throw jump. Alex literally threw Nikki into a double toe loop jump. The hardest part for Nikki would be to land solidly on one foot. She did it! Together, Nikki and Alex rounded the rink in time with the music and in time with each other. Their quick-footwork sequence of turns and crossovers was completely synchronized and brought cheers from the audience. Danielle was awed by how well they skated together in such a short amount of time.

The tempo of the music changed, and from where she was standing, Danielle could see Alex give Nikki a slight nod. She knew this meant they were about to perform their first lift, the dramatic star lift. Both

Nikki and Alex were skating backward and then suddenly Alex lifted Nikki with one hand on her waist and the other hand holding her hand. Amazingly Nikki was horizontal, high above Alex's head in a matter of seconds. Then Alex, the hours of weight-lifting having paid off, let go of Nikki's hand and supported her in the air with only one hand. The crowd went wild! Flashbulbs lit up the ice, and Danielle clapped enthusiastically for her friends. Nikki and Alex smiled widely as they completed the breathtaking lift and continued their program.

All too soon the pairs number ended. Danielle took a deep breath as she heard Mr. Ortega introduce her name over the public address system. This was it.

She shook her legs a little, adjusted the skirt of her skating costume, and skated out from backstage. The arena was completely dark.

Then a hot white spotlight flashed on as Danielle struck her opening pose. She blinked, then quickly regained her composure. She was going to follow Kathy's advice and try to forget about the TV cameras and the huge crowd. All she wanted to do was to skate her best.

Her music began, and Danielle pushed off into a graceful spiral, her leg extended high out behind her. The audience began to clap, and Danielle actually found herself smiling. This wasn't so bad, she told herself. In fact it was fun!

She moved through her program almost effortlessly. It was amazing how all the hours of practice had paid off. Her jumps were cleanly landed, her spins were centered, and she received a loud round of applause for her axel double-loop jump combination and her high, crowd-pleasing split jumps. Even her troublesome double Lutz jump went off without a hitch. Danielle was sure she heard Mr. Weiler give a victorious whoop from the bleachers, but she had no idea where he was sitting. Finally she placed a perfect spread eagle, a move in which she coasted across the rink on two outside edges with her arms above her head, right in front of the TV cameras.

By the time Danielle had finished her three-minute program, the crowd was on its feet, cheering. The whole routine had gone nearly perfectly!

The closing notes of her music were lost in all the clapping as Danielle continued to wave to the crowd. One of the little girls from the rock-lobster number came skating out with a big bunch of roses for her, and the bottom rows of the bleachers were crowded with kids waving their show programs for her to sign. Then the rest of the Silver Blades members skated out for the grand finale, and Danielle fell in behind them, still waving.

As she passed the section of the arena where she knew her family was sitting, she spotted her parents motioning to her frantically. "Great job!" her father called.

Grandma Panati was actually jumping up and down, holding a Silver Blades Skating Club banner. Jordan and Nicholas were waving their arms and making a lot of noise.

"All right, Tu—Danielle!" her brother hollered, catching himself just in time.

Danielle grinned and waved at the crowd. Right now she wouldn't even have cared if he had called her "Tubs."